"The Come to Me Love Spell should be used when you want to attract the attention of someone special," read Kate. "It will draw love to you and make you irresistible."

That could come in handy, she thought. At least it could if it were true. But there was no way something like that could work. You couldn't make people fall in love with you just by saying some words.

But what if you could? a voice in her mind asked. *What if you could make someone notice you? What if you could make* Scott *fall in love with you?*

Follow the Circle:

Book 2: Merry Meet
Book 3: Second Sight

circle of three

book 1

so mote it be

isobel bird

AVON BOOKS

An Imprint of HarperCollins*Publishers*

Library of Congress Catalog Card Number: 00-104541
ISBN: 0-06-447291-4

First Avon edition, 2001

❖

Visit us on the World Wide Web!
www.harperteen.com

CHAPTER I

"Okay, girls, listen up. Today is the twenty-eighth. That means we have a little more than two weeks to get organized. Does anyone have any ideas besides the tired old hearts-and-flowers thing? We have to announce the theme this week. How about you, Kate. Any thoughts?"

Kate Morgan looked up from her carton of blueberry yogurt, the spoon still in her mouth. Sherrie and the other girls were all looking at her, waiting for an answer, and she had no idea what the question was. She had been trying to get a look at Scott Coogan, who was sitting four tables over with the rest of the guys from the varsity football team. By turning her head she could just catch a glimpse of Scott, who was laughing at someone's joke, and she had been wondering what it would be like to sit with him and gaze into his blue, blue eyes.

"I'm sorry," Kate mumbled, swallowing her yogurt. "What were we talking about?"

Sherrie rolled her eyes and tossed her long,

curly black hair over her shoulder indignantly, the way she always did when she caught someone not listening to her. "The Valentine's Day dance," she said, as if the answer should be obvious. "You know, that little party we've been talking about for the past month? Maybe if you spent a little less time mooning over a certain dumb jock and paid more attention to us, your very best friends, you'd know what was going on."

Kate felt herself blushing. She'd thought she'd hidden her crush on Scott, but she should have known her friends would notice. By the smirks on their faces, she saw that they had.

"I'm not . . ." she started to say defensively, but they cut her off with shrieks of laughter.

"Come on," said Jessica mischievously. "We've seen the way you space out whenever he comes near you."

"Yeah," added Tara. "And whenever he passes your locker you suddenly forget your combination. Don't try to fool us. You've got it bad for that boy."

"Not that it will do you any good," said Sherrie, popping a potato chip into her mouth and looking very pleased with herself, as if she knew some vital piece of information they didn't know.

"Tell," said Jessica and Tara simultaneously.

"Well," said Sherrie dramatically, leaning over the table so she wouldn't have to talk too loudly. "After cheerleading practice yesterday I was in the locker room changing. You guys had already left—thank you very much for waiting, by the way—and the varsity team came in. I heard Linda Thomson telling Sarah Jennings that Scott is planning on asking Terri Fletcher to the dance. Linda is going out with Evan Markson, who, as you know, is Scott's best friend and—"

"We *know* who Evan Markson is," said Jessica, interrupting the story. "You aren't the only one around here who's up on the social scene at Beecher Falls High School."

"I was just citing the source," said Sherrie. "I'd hate to be accused of spreading false information."

"You and the *Enquirer*," Jessica teased.

"Terri Fletcher," said Tara thoughtfully, twirling a strand of her red hair around her finger. "She's that blond girl who played the lead in the drama club production last year, right?"

"Right," said Sherrie. "She's a junior."

"Scott would look good with her," said Tara, then she grimaced. "Sorry, Kate. I didn't mean you wouldn't look good with him or anything."

"Kate doesn't have a chance with Scott Coogan," said Sherrie decisively. "No offense, Kate. But look what you're up against. Terri's a junior. You're a sophomore. She's blond. You're blond-*ish*. She's a dainty little drama club girl. You're a jock. Clearly, Mr. Football likes them ditzy and helpless."

"Thanks for the reassurance," said Kate, wadding up her napkin and shoving it into her brown paper lunch bag. "I didn't realize I was so highly undatable."

"Relax," said Jessica, trying to smooth things over the way she always did when she felt someone getting upset. "You're gorgeous. I'd kill for your skin. We're just saying that clearly you're not what Scott is after. That's all."

"I don't know why we're even talking about this," Kate said angrily as she stood up from the table. "I don't care if he likes me or not any—"

She was cut off as she turned to leave and bumped into someone. The cup in her hand fell, splashing soda across the tabletop and onto Kate's shirt, soaking her.

"Sorry," said a male voice.

"Why don't you look where you're going?" Kate cried as she grabbed some napkins and dabbed at her shirt. She was already embarrassed by her friends' teasing, and now because of some guy's carelessness she was covered in soda. She looked up to see who had run into her, ready to give him a piece of her mind, and saw none other than Scott and his friends leaving the cafeteria without even a glance back at her. When she looked at her friends, they greeted her with we-told-you-so expressions.

"Now that *that* is out of the way, can we please talk about the dance?" asked Sherrie. "We can worry about who Kate's date is going to be once we decide on a theme."

"I need to go change my shirt," said Kate. "I'll

catch you guys later. That is, if you can stand to be seen with someone so deeply socially challenged."

Before any of them could protest, Kate walked toward the cafeteria doors. Tossing her lunch bag into the trash, she stormed into the hallway and made her way to the girls' locker room. Being a member of the junior varsity basketball team meant that she had her own locker, and she was pretty sure she'd left an extra shirt in it. Besides, she wanted to be alone for a few minutes. She generally didn't stay mad for long, but when she was upset she hated to be around other people.

The locker room was empty, and Kate was relieved to see that there was indeed another shirt in her locker, right there beside the one she wore for practice. It was a white, long-sleeved oxford she'd stolen from her older brother, Kyle, the last time he was home from college, but it would have to do. Removing her sticky T-shirt, she pulled on the fresh shirt and buttoned it up, leaving it untucked. Shoving the dirty T-shirt into her gym bag, she slammed the locker door more forcefully than she meant to and sat down on the long wooden bench that ran between the two rows of lockers. There was a full-length mirror attached to the wall at the end of the row, and she stared angrily at her reflection in it.

Why did I get stuck with such boring looks? she thought to herself. Her shoulder-length mousy hair was pulled back into the ponytail that she wore to keep it out of her face while she was playing ball. She wished it was curly, like Sherrie's, or dramatically red, like Tara's. She imagined herself with straight blond hair and startling blue eyes, like Jessica had, or with Tara's freckled Irish complexion. *Anything but plain old brownish hair and grayish eyes*, she thought.

She knew she was just indulging in a little self-pity, but she was still smarting from their comments about her and Scott. The truth was, she was just as pretty as her friends were. Her body, lean from all the sports she played, certainly wasn't as filled out as the bodies of some other girls. But she looked good, even in old jeans and an oversized men's shirt.

So why did her friends just assume that a boy like Scott Coogan would never consider going out with her? What was it about her that made the idea of them together so hard to believe? They appeared to be right, though, judging from the fact that she didn't seem to register on Scott's radar, even when he bumped into her. Thinking about how he'd walked away with only a mumbled apology made her even more depressed and angry.

It wasn't like she wasn't popular. She had lots of friends, both on the team and off. She and her three best friends had even been elected to the social events committee of student government, and now they were planning the big Valentine's Day dance together. She was always going to parties, and tons of guys noticed her. So why was she so upset that one guy out of the entire school wasn't paying attention to her? Why did she have to have a thing for him anyway? She didn't even really know him. It was just something about him. It was such a cliché, the sophomore girl falling for the senior football player. She felt stupid even thinking about it.

The ringing of the bell for sixth period interrupted her thoughts. Gathering up her books, she left the gym and walked to her next class. It was history with Mr. Draper, and she wasn't looking forward to it. Today was the day they had to tell him what the topics for their term papers were, and she still had no idea what she was going to do hers on. History was far from her favorite subject, and the period they were studying—Europe in the sixteenth century—was nothing to get excited about.

She made it to class just as the second bell was ringing. Slipping into her seat, she hoped maybe Mr. Draper would forget about the paper topics and spend the forty-five minutes showing them slides of ancient castles or something so that she could think about other things.

But he hadn't forgotten. As soon as everyone had settled down, Mr. Draper closed the door and faced them. "Okay," he said. "Term paper topics."

There was a collective groan as everyone slid down in their seats, hoping they wouldn't be called on.

"Please," said Mr. Draper, holding his hand over his chest as if he were having a heart attack. "Don't show so much enthusiasm. I don't think I can take it."

Kate smiled in spite of herself. Even though she didn't find his class very interesting, she liked Mr. Draper. He was young—just out of college—and he didn't treat his students like they were stupid. He couldn't help it if he was stuck teaching the most boring subject in the tenth grade.

"Does *anyone* have a topic picked out?" asked Mr. Draper hopefully.

A couple of hands went up tentatively. Mr. Draper called on those students one at a time and wrote down the topic each one had selected. When he was done, he picked up a box that was sitting on his desk.

"I suspected there might be some of you who wouldn't be able to choose from among all the thrilling possibilities available to you," he said, getting a laugh from the class. "So I took the liberty of drawing up some ideas."

He handed the box to the girl at the head of the first row of desks. "Inside this box are pieces of paper with various topics written on them," he explained. "Those of you who haven't chosen a topic may pick one at random out of the box."

"What if we don't like the topic?" asked Jerry Hoban doubtfully.

"If you could think of one you liked better,

Jerry, you wouldn't be picking one out of a box," said Mr. Draper.

The first girl reached into the box and pulled out a piece of paper. "The life of Shakespeare," she read, sounding relieved as she passed the box to the next person.

As the box went down the line, Kate listened to the topics chosen by the other students. Suddenly they all seemed fascinating, and she wondered why she hadn't thought to write about the beheading of Anne Boleyn, Magellan's explorations, or the excommunication of Queen Elizabeth I. When the box was passed to her, she hesitated for a moment and then reached inside. Grabbing a piece of paper, she drew it out and opened it.

"The witchcraft persecutions," she read, frowning.

As the box continued around the room and others chose their topics, Kate kept looking at the slip of paper in her hand. She didn't really know anything about witches, although the class had briefly discussed the fact that a lot of people had been tried and executed for participating in witchcraft during the Inquisition. Writing a report on the subject was going to mean a lot of work, and what with basketball and planning the Valentine's Day dance and everything else she had to do, she didn't have a lot of time to be hanging out in the library.

The box reached the end of the last row, and finally everyone had a topic. A couple of people traded, but no one offered to take Kate's topic, so she was stuck with it. Mr. Draper spent the rest of the period going over material for their upcoming midterm, so Kate was able to zone out and daydream about what she was going to wear to the Valentine's Day dance. Not that it mattered if she didn't have a date. That thought made her even more miserable, so she just sat and drew meaningless pictures in her notebook until the bell rang.

Kate's next period was phys ed. Because she was on the basketball team, she got to spend her time in the gym practicing with other members of the team who had p.e. then too. When she arrived, Tara and Jessica were practicing free throws along with a few other girls. Kate changed into shorts and her practice T-shirt and joined them.

"You in a better mood?" Jessica asked as she tossed Kate a ball.

"Give me a few minutes and I will be," Kate said as she attempted a shot and watched the ball bounce off the rim. "Or maybe I won't."

"Still mooning over jock boy?" her friend teased.

"No, it's Mr. Draper," Kate answered, retrieving the ball.

"I don't think Mr. Draper would go with you to the dance," Tara commented. "But it's a nice thought."

"Cute," said Kate, making another throw and feeling slightly better when the ball swished through the net. "I got a lame topic for his term paper."

"It can't be any worse than trying to come up with an idea Sherrie likes for the dance," said Jessica. "She's been on a rampage since lunch."

"That's Sherrie," said Kate. "She *lives* for planning things like this. Once she picks something, she'll be fine. You know she always asks us for ideas and then does exactly what she wants to anyway."

"I know," said Tara. "But now she's talking about doing some kind of doomed lovers theme. You know, Romeo and Juliet, Anthony and Cleopatra, those whiners from *Titanic*. We have to stop her."

"We'll talk her out of it," said Kate, taking the ball and passing it to Jessica.

"We'll get a chance after school," Jessica said. "She wants us to meet at her house when she's done with cheerleading."

"Maybe," Kate said as the ball returned to her. "I've got to go to the library and do some research for Draper's paper. It's going to take a while."

"Are you hoping to run into Scott?" Jessica asked slyly.

"Like he'd be in the library," Kate replied sarcastically. "Besides, Jess, as you all pointed out so thoroughly at lunch, I'm most definitely not his type." She'd pretty much forgiven her friends for their comments, but she was still stung by the truth of them, and she really wanted to change the subject. "Let's just play," she said.

The girls formed two teams, and moments later

Kate was racing down the court, her mind emptied of everything except the way the ball was moving and where the other players were. As the game went on, Kate forgot about Scott and about her history paper. The score was close, but just as the bell signaling the end of the period rang, Kate sank the shot that carried her team over the edge. She felt great as they went into the locker room to shower and change. As she walked out of the gym with Jessica and Tara, she felt as if the day wasn't nearly as bad as she'd thought it was forty-five minutes before. Kate's last period class was study hall, but the library was an option when needed, so that's where she headed.

"We'll be at Sherrie's if you finish early," Jessica told her as they parted at the library doors. "See you later."

Kate went into the library and put her backpack on a table in a corner. Going over to one of the computers, she sat down and started to search for anything she could find on her assigned history topic. Typing "witchcraft" into the search engine, she waited to see what the library's collection would come up with. To her surprise, there were quite a number of books on the list. She jotted down their locations and went to find them.

Seated on the floor between the shelves, Kate scanned the row of books in front of her, reading some of the titles: *Witchcraft Through the Ages, The Devil's Hiding Place, The Witch Trials of*

Europe. There were more books than she had expected to find, and she didn't know where to start. Eventually she pulled a book out at random and flipped through it. It was filled with old engravings of people being burned at the stake, hung from gallows, and tied to strange torture devices. The images made her uncomfortable, and she quickly shut the book and picked up another one.

For the next half hour Kate browsed the books, trying to decide if witchcraft was something she could write about. Some of the stuff she found seemed sort of interesting, but nothing really grabbed her. Plus her left leg was asleep from sitting on the floor. She stood up and tried to walk it out. As she stumbled out from the shelves, the library doors opened and two people came in, talking loudly. When she saw Scott Coogan coming toward her with Evan Markson, her heart jumped in her chest. Suddenly, everything bad about the day came back to her, and Scott was the last person she wanted to see. All she wanted to do was get out of the library and go home. Gathering up the books around her, and ignoring the monstrous pins-and-needles traveling up and down her left leg, she carried them as quickly as she could to the front desk to check them out.

"Looks like you're doing a paper," the person behind the desk said as she took the circulation cards out of the books and stamped them with a due date.

"Yeah, it's for my history class," Kate answered, glancing up. When she saw who it was, she froze. Of all the people she didn't want to see, she'd thought Scott was number one. Now she realized he was number two—next to his alleged dream girl, Terri Fletcher. As Kate stared at Terri, all she could think was that she would never be as pretty as her, that Scott would never ask her out, and that she was a social failure. Then, to make things worse, she heard Scott's voice coming toward her.

"Could you hurry?" she said, anxiously watching Terri stamp each book methodically. "I really need to get home."

"I'm almost done," Terri said. "Just one more to go." She stamped the last card, put the book on top of the others, and pushed the stack toward Kate. "There you go."

"Thanks," Kate said hurriedly. She picked up the pile of books and moved away from the desk as quickly as she could, trying to keep her back to Scott. She didn't want to bump into him again—and, even more, she didn't want to see him smiling at Terri.

Dumping the books into her backpack and grabbing her coat, Kate took off, deliberately not glancing at the circulation desk, where Scott was leaning over the counter, talking to Terri. Instead, she focused on the doors as if they were the net in a basketball game. The goal was to get to them and out into the hallway without looking anywhere but straight ahead.

When she felt the door handle beneath her fingers, she pushed hard and practically burst into the hallway. Then she ran down the hall to the front doors and out into the cold January afternoon. As she began her walk through town and toward home, she couldn't help but think about how she wished she was the one Scott had come into the library to talk to instead of Terri. As much as she hated to admit it, her friends were right. She would give almost anything to have him be interested in her. If only she could find some way to make him notice her.

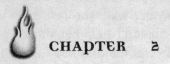

CHAPTER 2

"Hello?" Kate called out as she shut the front door of her house behind her.

There was no answer. Kate hung her coat in the hall closet and looked into the living room, but it was empty except for the tools her father never managed to put away. Although they'd lived in the old house on Halifax Street since before Kate was born, her father was always finding something else to fix or restore. At the moment he was repairing the tiles around the fireplace, and there was a mess all over the floor. The dining room was empty as well. But in the kitchen Kate found a note from her mother on the counter.

Kate:
I'm catering a party this evening and your father is work-
ing late at the store. Dinner's in the fridge. Hope you like
it. We should both be home by 10:00.
Love,
Mom

Normally, Kate loved having dinner with her parents. Unlike some of her friends, she got along really well with her family. She liked telling them about her day as they ate together, and she enjoyed hearing her mother talk about her catering business and laughing at her father's good-natured complaining about the neophyte hikers and cell phone–toting outdoor enthusiasts who flocked to his sporting goods store to get outfitted for their trips into the forests that surrounded Beecher Falls. But tonight she was happy to have the house to herself so she wouldn't have to answer any questions. As much as she liked her parents, she didn't want to talk to them about how awful she was feeling over what had happened at school.

Kate peeked into the fridge, saw that her mother had left her some pasta salad and chicken for dinner, and grabbed a soda to take up to her room with her. Upstairs, she put a CD into the stereo, took off her shoes, and flopped onto her bed. Outside the window the sky was gray and stormy, which was exactly how she felt herself.

She opened her backpack and dumped the library books onto her bed. She'd been in such a hurry to get out of the library that she hadn't even really looked at which books she'd grabbed. Now she went through them, hoping one of them would give her something to work with. It looked as though she was going to have to find out all she could about witchcraft, whether she liked it or not.

She picked up the first book and started reading. At first she found it difficult going because there were a lot of dates and numbers, and the style was dry. But the longer she read, the more interested she became. According to the book, hundreds of thousands of people had been tried as witches in Europe during the fifteenth and sixteenth centuries. Many of them had confessed to being witches after enduring horrible tortures, and most ended up being executed anyway.

The more she read, the more Kate found it incredible that anyone would believe the stories told by the people who accused others of being witches. Flying through the air? Talking to the Devil? Making people die? None of it made any sense. Yet thousands and thousands of people had died because someone *did* believe that they were witches and could do these things. People had been so frightened by the idea that witches existed and had terrible powers that in some villages in Europe entire populations had been wiped out.

There was definitely enough material for her to write a paper. Relieved, she shut the book she was reading and put it back on the pile. She'd been reading for a long time and was feeling more than a little hungry, especially since she'd left most of her lunch uneaten. She decided to get the dinner her mother had left her and get back to the books later. Now that she knew there was enough for a report, she wasn't in such a hurry.

As she got off the bed, she knocked the pile of books over and they fell onto the floor. She bent down to pick them up, and the cover of one of them caught her eye. It had a picture of a woman sitting behind a burning candle, and it was called *Spells and Charms for the Modern Witch*. She didn't remember choosing it at the library. *I must have grabbed it by mistake*, she thought as she picked it up and opened it.

Unlike the other books, this one wasn't a history book. It appeared to be an actual book of spells and rituals. The contents page listed all kinds of weird things, like charms for warding off evil, rituals for bringing good luck, and directions for making potions. It all sounded like a bunch of nonsense, but Kate found herself leafing through the pages anyway.

There were some photographs in the book of people doing the different spells and rituals. Unlike the creepy engravings in the other books, these photos showed normal-looking women and men. They weren't wearing pointy hats or black capes or anything. Some were dressed in plain old jeans and T-shirts. They didn't look much different from the people Kate might see at the mall—or even at church on Sunday mornings. As she looked at their faces, Kate wondered if they were really witches. She would have expected them to look different somehow, but they looked just like her.

She turned to one of the spells and started

reading. It was a spell to cleanse a place of negative energy. She was surprised to see that there were no complicated rhymes or incantations. In fact, the spell didn't seem difficult at all. It just involved lighting some candles, doing some kind of meditation, and saying a few words. Anyone could do it.

Kate was sort of disappointed. From her few impressions of witchcraft, she'd expected spells to be at least a little bit spooky. But the ones in the book sounded about as easy and mysterious as making Jell-O—just add hot water and wait. There were no strange ingredients, and the book didn't say anything about having to do the spells in a secret place in the woods or under a full moon or anything like that. The woman in the picture that accompanied the cleansing spell was doing it in her living room.

Anyone could do that, Kate thought. Then she had another thought: *I could do that if I wanted to.* The idea of trying to perform a spell herself made her laugh. She'd feel so silly sitting in front of a candle, saying the words of the spell, and waiting for something to happen. Besides, she was no witch. She was just plain old Kate Morgan, who needed to do a report for school. This wasn't really her kind of thing at all.

Leaving the book on her bed, she went down to the kitchen and took out her dinner. A quick three minutes in the microwave had the chicken smelling like it was fresh from the oven, and Kate sat down at the table to enjoy her mother's cooking. As she ate, she found herself thinking about the people accused of witchcraft by the witch-hunters. What would she have done if she'd been accused of witchcraft? Would she have proclaimed her innocence, as so many of them did despite being tortured, or would she have confessed in the hope that she might be spared? Would she, if pressed, have accused other people of being witches, even if she knew it wasn't true?

She couldn't even imagine being in that situation. She couldn't understand what it was about witches, or even just the idea of witches, that made people so upset that they would torture and kill one another in such terrible ways. But then she thought about her reaction to the book of spells. Just looking at it had made her a little uncomfortable. Why? Was it because she was afraid that witches might really exist and that witchcraft might not be just stories and legends? The people in the photos had looked just like her, but she couldn't ever imagine calling herself a witch. She didn't even know what made someone a witch. In her church, people were confirmed by a priest. She wondered if witches had some kind of similar ceremony, or if you just decided you were a witch and that made you one. But if anyone could do it, why couldn't she? Maybe she could. She found the idea both strangely exciting and distinctly upsetting.

She finished her dinner and washed the dishes. Then she returned to her room. Avoiding the book of spells, she opened one of the others and started to read more about the witch persecutions. But her mind kept wandering back to the book on the floor beside the bed. Finally, after she'd read the same paragraph over three times without remembering a word of it, she gave in. Tossing aside the book she was reading, she picked up the spell book and opened it.

She didn't have any intention of trying any of the spells. But she was curious about what else was in the book. She read through a few more spells; they all seemed similar to the one she had read earlier. Then she turned the page and saw something called the "Come to Me Love Spell." Intrigued by the suggestive title, she started reading it.

"The Come to Me Love Spell should be used when you want to attract the attention of someone special," she read. "It will draw love to you and make you irresistible."

That could come in handy, Kate thought. At least it could if it were true. But there was no way something like that could work. You couldn't make people fall in love with you just by saying some words.

But what if you could? a voice in her mind asked. *What if you could make someone notice you? What if you could make* Scott *fall in love with you?*

Suddenly, Kate was looking at the Come to Me Love Spell differently. Could she really do it? Could she actually make Scott Coogan notice her, even fall in love with her, just by doing a spell in a book? She wasn't even a witch. Would a spell work if just anybody did it? Kate didn't know. It seemed so ridiculous.

But what have you got to lose? the voice in her head asked.

"Nothing," Kate said out loud, surprising herself. But it was true. She didn't have anything to lose by trying out the spell. If nothing happened, she wouldn't be any worse off than she already was. And if it did work . . . she couldn't let herself think about that.

Skipping the rest of the introduction, Kate went right to the directions for working the spell, before she could change her mind. She looked at the list of things she would need. She was pretty sure she had everything right there in the house, and she ran downstairs to look for the first two things—some red candles and some matches. Luckily, there were a number of small votive candles on the fireplace mantel, left over from the Christmas arrangement her mother had made, and Kate gathered them and carried them upstairs after grabbing some matches from the junk drawer in the kitchen. She made a detour to her mother's sewing room and returned with a piece of red construction paper, a black marker, and some red ribbon from the well-stocked box of craft items her Martha Stewart–obsessed mother kept.

Even though she was alone in the house, Kate

shut her door. Part of her was still worried that someone would walk in on her, and she felt silly enough trying out a spell from a witchcraft book without having to explain to her parents what she was doing if they came home early and surprised her. They were pretty cool as far as letting her do her own thing, but she had a feeling this was something they would definitely not understand.

She put the candles on the floor and looked at the spell again. She had almost everything on the list. But the last item was a problem. The book said she needed something that represented the person whose attention she wanted to attract. "You might want to use a photo, or even make a doll out of a piece of clothing belonging to the object of your affection," she read. But there was no way for her to get something that belonged to Scott, and she didn't have any pictures of him.

She was about to abandon the idea and put everything back, but then she had an idea. In her closet was a bag filled with the dolls she'd played with when she was younger. Dragging it out, she pawed through the assorted Barbies and Skippers until she found what she was looking for—a Ken doll. With its blond hair and blue eyes, it looked sort of like Scott. It was even wearing a letterman jacket like the one he wore.

"You'll be perfect," she said to the doll as she threw the others back into the closet.

Then it was time to go to work. She picked up

the book and read the directions: "Arrange the seven small candles (or more if you like) around you in a circle."

She cleared a space in the middle of the room, pushing her clothes, shoes, and assorted books and papers aside. Then she arranged the seven red candles in a circle, leaving enough room to sit inside the circle without being too close to the candles. Before sitting down, she turned off the bedroom light. Once she was surrounded by the darkness, she felt a little bit afraid. What was she doing? Was it dangerous? For a moment she was tempted to turn the light back on and forget about the whole thing. It was silly anyway. But another part of her, a more insistent, curious part, wanted to see what would happen.

"Light the circle of candles," she read, holding the book close to her face in the milky darkness. "As you do, imagine yourself sitting in a circle of bright light."

Kate struck a match and lit the candles one at a time. As the circle grew, the room filled with a soft warm glow. *So far, so good*, she thought to herself as she read the next step.

Following the directions, she cut a heart shape out of the red paper and, using the marker, wrote her own name on it. Then, holding the Ken doll in one hand, she pressed the heart with her name on it against his chest and held it there. Then she took the red ribbon and began to wind it around the doll, starting at the feet and moving up the body. As she wound the ribbon, tying the heart to the doll, she spoke the words of the spell.

> *With this ribbon I do bind*
> *my heart to yours and yours to mine.*
> *Love, I call you, come to me,*
> *As is my will, so mote it be.*

She said the words three times, each time a little more loudly. On the final "so mote it be," she tied the ribbon firmly across the doll's chest and knotted it. It was now wrapped up like a caterpillar in a cocoon, with only its head visible. Its smiling plastic face beamed up at her stupidly.

I guess that's it, Kate thought. She found herself giggling nervously, like a little kid. *I just did a spell.* It all seemed so silly. She hadn't done anything but light some candles and play with a doll. She didn't see how that could possibly have an effect on whether Scott would notice her or not. Plus, she didn't even know when it would kick in, since the disclaimer at the bottom of the spell very clearly stated, "Effects may take up to forty-eight hours to appear. Results may vary." But it had been kind of fun.

She looked at the clock on her bedside table. Her parents would be home any minute. Standing up, she turned on the bedroom light. Then she blew out the candles. She couldn't put them back, because her mother would notice that they had been used and ask why. Instead, she put them into an empty shoe box. She wasn't sure what she should do with the doll, so she stuck it in the shoe box with the candles and put the box in the back of her closet. She would figure out what to do with everything later, but for the moment she didn't want anyone stumbling upon it accidentally. She had just closed the closet door when she heard the downstairs door open.

"Kate?" her father called. "Are you home, honey?"

Kate opened her bedroom door and went downstairs. Both her parents were there, taking off their coats.

"I stopped by the store after my party and forced your father to come home," her mother said. "If I hadn't, I think he would have just set up camp in one of the display tents."

"Hi, Daddy," Kate said. "Was the store busy today?"

"Very," he said. "We had a bunch of winter campers come in. They're all heading up to Olympia National Park for some snowshoeing this weekend and needed gear."

"How was the party?" she asked her mother.

"The shrimp puffs were a little too toasty, but I don't think anyone noticed but me," she answered. "And what did you do tonight?"

Kate wondered what they would say if she told

them, "Oh, I tried out this witchcraft spell. No big deal." Instead she said, "Just some school stuff." Technically it was true, so she didn't feel bad about not being completely honest.

She stayed downstairs for a while and talked to her parents. Then it was time for bed. Back upstairs, Kate changed into the old T-shirt she liked to sleep in and got into bed. As she lay in the darkness with her quilt pulled up around her, she thought about the doll in her closet. Maybe she hadn't worked any magic. After all, she'd just lit some candles and said a simple rhyme. No one could call that playing with supernatural powers or anything. People lit candles all the time, even in church, and it had nothing to do with magic or spells.

Still, part of her hoped that maybe there was more to it than that. As she drifted off, she imagined herself sitting in a circle of lit candles, saying some words she couldn't quite make out. Then she saw a figure walking toward her. It looked like a guy. But before she could see his face, she was asleep.

CHAPTER 3

The next morning as she walked to school Kate tried to imagine what it would be like if Scott really *did* ask her to the dance. She tried out several different scenarios, but the one she liked best involved her standing by her locker, putting her books away, and Scott coming up and gently touching her shoulder. She saw herself turning around and looking into his blue eyes. She watched as he smiled, opened his mouth, and said, "Hey, Kate."

That's not very romantic, she thought. Then she realized that it wasn't just her imagination—someone really had spoken to her. She looked up and saw that Jeff Higdon was standing in front of her on the steps of the school.

"Um, hey, Jeff," she said, her breath making little clouds in the morning air. Like Scott, Jeff was also on the football team. And like Scott, he had never spoken to Kate before. But now he was acting as if they talked to one another all the time.

"So, how are you today?" he asked, sounding

nervous as he stood with his hands in his jeans pockets.

Kate looked around, wondering if maybe Jeff and some of his buddies were playing a joke on her. But nothing seemed out of the ordinary, except that Jeff was watching her expectantly, waiting for an answer.

"I'm fine," she said, and there was a long pause.

"Um, did you want something?" she said finally.

Jeff shook his head. "No," he said. "Nothing special. I just wanted to say hey and, you know, see how you are."

"Well, thanks, I guess," Kate said. "But I'm getting kind of cold. I guess I'll just go to my locker now. See you later."

She walked past Jeff and into the building. As she went down the hall toward her locker, it seemed like several people's eyes were on her. She couldn't say exactly why, but she felt as if she was being watched. Only when she turned around to see who was looking at her, all she saw were guys walking quickly toward their classrooms.

As Kate took her books out of her locker, she heard someone come up behind her. She turned around hopefully, thinking that it might really be Scott. But it was only Sherrie, Jessica, and Tara.

"Thanks for all your help yesterday."

"Hey, guys," Kate said. "I'm sorry. I had so much homework to do that I just couldn't make it." She felt guilty for not telling her friends what she'd really been doing, but she was starting to feel a little silly about the whole thing, and she knew she'd feel even dumber if she had to talk about it.

"It's a sad day when studying is more important than social commitments," Sherrie said, only half joking. "But we'll forgive you."

"This time," added Tara.

"Besides," said Jessica, "we came up with a totally brilliant idea."

Kate shut her locker. "Oh, yeah?" she said, glad to have a change of subject. "What is it? No, let me guess—a masquerade ball?"

All three of them glared at her.

"How did you know?" demanded Sherrie.

"It took us three hours to come up with that," said Tara.

Kate smiled. "Then I guess you didn't need me after all," she said. "But it was just a lucky guess. Is that really what you decided to do?"

"Well, we *did* think it was original," said Jessica. "But clearly if *you* came up with it in two seconds it isn't."

"Maybe she just has highly developed psychic powers," suggested Tara.

"Or maybe she's a witch," said Sherrie.

"Why did you say that?" Kate snapped.

"Relax," said Sherrie, taking Kate by the arm. "I'm just trying to explain your amazing powers of deduction. They have us mere mortals mystified."

"Sorry," Kate said. "I guess I just wish I'd been

there with you guys instead of home with a bunch of books."

"I keep telling you that too much reading is going to get you into trouble one of these days," Sherrie said. "But on to better things.

"I'm thinking palace ballroom for the motif," she said as they walked. "We'll turn the gym into Sleeping Beauty's castle. Not the thorn-covered, nasty one—the one they hold the celebration in after the prince wakes her up. Lots of pink and white, and the whole ceiling strung with white Christmas lights."

"Oh, and when couples enter we'll announce their names, just like at a fancy dress ball," said Tara excitedly.

"Like you've been to so many that you would know about that," sniped Sherrie.

"You're not the only one who saw *Shakespeare in Love*," Tara replied. "Just imagine everyone lined up, and then the announcer says, 'Ladies and gentlemen, may I present Tara Redding and Al Dillinger.'"

"Al Dillinger?" Kate, Sherrie, and Jessica said in one voice, stopping in the middle of the hall and looking at their friend.

"He asked me this morning," Tara said, her freckles turning pink under her friends' scrutiny. "And I said yes."

Al Dillinger was a quiet guy who spent most of his time in the art room, painting or working on some kind of sculpture that never seemed to get finished. None of them had ever heard him say more than a few words to anyone, especially not to any of them.

"It's those quiet ones you have to look out for," said Sherrie knowingly.

"I was surprised, too," said Tara. "It took him forever to get the question out."

"Well, that's one down," said Kate.

"Two," said Sherrie. "I didn't want to say anything, because none of you had dates yet, but Sean asked me if I would go with him."

Unlike Tara's announcement, Sherrie's was no big shock. Sean McNeeley and Sherrie had gone out a couple of times, and it was no secret that they liked each other. Sherrie just wasn't ready to instate him as her boyfriend because, as she'd said, she owed it to the male student population not to get tied down so early in her high school career.

"I guess that just leaves you and me, Jess," Kate said, putting her arm around her friend. "So what do you say we just go together and cause a scandal? We could go as Catwoman and Batgirl."

"Sorry," said Jessica. "Much as I'd love to don a slinky latex number, I already told Blair I'd go with him."

"Blair?" said Sherrie incredulously. "That's like going with your brother."

Blair Peterson had been Jessica's neighbor since they were both six years old. They'd been best friends until the onset of adolescence made them both a little embarrassed about it, but they still hung out a lot, and most people just assumed they were an item. No matter how many times Jessica explained that she hung out with Blair because they both played cello in the school orchestra, no one believed her.

"Since there was asking involved, can we safely say that this time you're on an official date?" said Tara, bringing up an old group joke. Neither Jessica nor Blair had ever gone out with anyone else, and both routinely turned down offers from other people, but they refused to call what they did together dating. Jessica, as usual, ignored the question, tucking her hair behind her ears deliberately and pretending to examine the floor's industrial linoleum.

"That just leaves you, Kate," she said, trying to deflect the conversation away from the topic of her and Blair.

"And no, you can't go alone," Sherrie said before Kate could say anything. "You're going with a boy, and that's that. We can't have a member of the planning committee going solo."

Kate sighed. Talking about dates only reminded her of Scott and the dates they were *not* having, and that was something she most definitely did not want to think about.

"I'll work on it," she said feebly.

"Al's friend Dan needs a date," suggested Tara. "I

could ask him if he wants to go with you."

"Not Dan who runs the projectors for the AV department?" said Sherrie dismissively. "Please, Tar, Kate hasn't yet sunk to the level of mercy dating."

"He's a nice guy," Tara said defensively. "I think he'd clean up just fine."

"Can we not talk about this anymore?" Kate said. "I said I'd handle the date situation."

"Just don't wait too long," said Sherrie. "The more days go by, the closer you are to AV guy."

Any further discussion was cut short by the ringing of the bell. But Sherrie had to get in one final dig. "And don't even think about holding out for Scott," she said as she and Jessica headed off, leaving Kate and Tara to their chemistry class. "You'd need Sleeping Beauty's fairy godmothers and their magic wands to make that happen."

Kate didn't have much time to think about the dance during chemistry. In preparation for their midterm the next day, Miss Blackwood was having them do a practice experiment. Kate followed Tara to their usual lab station, but she noticed that wherever she went the boys in the class were watching her, some openly and some only when they thought she wasn't looking.

"Maybe I put too much into it," she said, suddenly thinking about last night's spell, not realizing that she was talking out loud.

"Too much what?" asked Tara, shaking a spoonful

of greenish powder from the bottle in her hand into a measuring spoon.

"Oh, nothing," said Kate. "How much water do we need to add to that?"

Kate went to the sink to fill a beaker with water. She couldn't help but notice that all the boys watched her as she passed by. One, distracted from his experiment, added the water to the wrong flask and started choking as the reaction produced a thick cloud of smoke.

"Watch it, Tony," said his partner, grabbing the smoking container and dumping it into a nearby sink.

"Sorry, Annie," Tony said sheepishly, not taking his eyes off Kate. "I got distracted."

Annie Crandall followed Tony's gaze, and when she saw Kate she frowned. "Save that kind of chemistry for after class," she said, giving Kate a hard look. "I don't want to blow this practical tomorrow."

"What are you worried about?" Tony said, watching Kate as she walked back to her table. "You always ace this stuff."

Tony's right, Kate thought as she read over the instructions for the experiment. *Annie does always get A's in chemistry.* In fact, Kate wished that she could do half as well as Annie Crandall did.

Kate and Tara did their best to make their experiment work out, but something seemed to be not quite right about it. The liquid in their test tube turned bright purple instead of green, and it gave off an awful smell. Oddly, other groups seemed to be getting similar results—especially groups with at least one male partner. They all seemed to be distracted by something, and more and more that something appeared to be Kate.

"Let me help you with that," said Billy Himler as Kate carried her and Tara's failed experiment to the sink.

"No, let me," said Peter James, trying to take the dirty beakers from Kate's hands. Unfortunately, he only succeeded in making her lose her grip, and the containers crashed to the floor and shattered.

"Steer clear of the chemicals!" ordered Miss Blackwood, coming over to see what was going on. "What happened here?"

"The guys were just trying to help me," Kate tried to explain.

"Well, now they can help you clean up this mess," Miss Blackwood said. "Be sure to pick up all the glass."

Billy and Peter practically fell down in their rush to come to Kate's aid. They were joined by a couple of other boys, and soon the floor was wiped clean again.

"I don't know what you're up to, but whatever it is, it's working," Tara said to Kate as they watched the boys throw out the last of the glass.

"I have no idea what this is all about," Kate said.

But she did know what it was about. The spell

was working overtime. She didn't know how or why, but instead of making just one boy interested in her, it seemed to have made *all* the boys interested in her. Wherever she looked, another guy was watching her. It made her feel a little nervous, but it also made her feel really good. She felt powerful. She'd done a spell, and it was really working.

"If your performances today are any indication, you're all going to be in big trouble tomorrow," Miss Blackwood said from the front of the room, bringing Kate's thoughts back to the class. "I suggest you spend tonight studying, because this midterm counts for one third of your final grade."

Kate gathered up her notebooks, and she and Tara left the classroom. As they walked down the hallway, they found themselves tailed by several boys. Kate also couldn't help but notice that Annie Crandall scowled at her and turned away as she passed by. But she quickly forgot about Annie as the group of boys continued to follow her and Tara.

"Okay, back off," Tara said finally, turning around and standing between her friend and the group of boys. "I don't know what's gotten into you boys today, but give us a little room here. The lady needs to breathe."

One by one the guys turned and reluctantly walked off, and soon Kate and Tara were walking by themselves again.

"I swear they're all just walking hormones," Tara said as they made their way to their next class.

"Word must have gotten out that you're looking for a date for the dance."

"That must be it," Kate said, hoping Tara would drop the subject. She was excited about all the attention the boys were paying to her, but the one boy she really wanted to notice her hadn't even made an appearance. But why, when she had specifically focused on him? She was starting to worry that she'd done something wrong and the spell had backfired. She tried to remember exactly what she'd said when she did it, but it was all running together in her head.

As they turned the corner, the two girls saw Jessica and Sherrie standing in the hall ahead of them. Jessica was holding a poster against the wall, and Sherrie was directing her on where to put it.

"A little higher," she said as Kate and Tara approached. "Now to the left. That's perfect."

Jessica taped the poster in place and stepped back to admire her work.

"Looks good," Kate said.

"Only nineteen more to go," Sherrie said, handing her a roll of tape. "Why don't you come with me and we'll do the second floor. Tara and Jess can do the rest of this floor."

"What about class?" Kate said.

Sherrie waved a handful of paper slips at her. "Passes," she said. "We're on official student government business. Now, follow me."

Before Kate could protest, Sherrie started for

the stairs. Leaving Tara and Jessica, Kate followed, tape in hand.

"I figure we should put three in each hallway and one in the other stairwell," Sherrie said as she walked ahead of Kate. "Jess and I already put some by the gym, the art rooms, and the library, so that should cover everything. So, have you thought any more about your date?"

"Not really," said Kate. Sherrie hadn't witnessed any of the Kate-induced craziness that had overtaken the guys yet, and for once Kate was thankful for the fact that her friend was so self-involved. While Tara seemed to be taking Kate's newfound popularity as some kind of freak accident, Kate knew that Sherrie would be suspicious, and she didn't know how long she could hold out under the interrogation she was sure to get. She told her friends absolutely everything, but this spell stuff was one thing she didn't think she could share with them. She didn't understand it herself. *Besides,* she thought as she remembered the way the boys had fallen all over themselves in chemistry class, *I like being the one who gets noticed for a change.*

"I'm only telling you this for your own good," Sherrie said as they stopped outside Mr. Draper's room to hang a poster. "But it's high time you started paying more attention to your romantic life. I know you and Jess and Tara think the basketball team is the most important thing in the world, but there *is* life off the court."

"Thanks for reminding me," Kate said as she pulled off a piece of tape. "Is this straight?"

"Yes," said Sherrie. "I'm just saying that maybe you should think about, you know, developing a more well-rounded personality."

"Says the girl who thinks cheerleading should count for academic credit," Kate shot back.

"Well, it does combine athletic skills with linguistic ability," Sherrie answered primly. "But we're not talking about me. We're talking about you."

"That's a refreshing change," said Kate, "but let's not." She picked up the posters and moved on. Of all her friends, only Sherrie had a way of making her feel like a total social disaster. She always had, ever since they'd met on the first day of second grade and Sherrie had immediately taken charge of Kate's untied shoelace and crooked barrette. Somehow they'd managed to stay friends, but sometimes Kate wished she could do something to show Sherrie up once and for all, to prove that she was just as popular as Sherrie was, or thought she was. Just once she wished she could be the girl everyone else envied.

They were standing at the end of the hall, putting a poster on the wall where everyone going up or down the stairs would see it. Sherrie had launched into a long speech about how Kate would look so much better if she would just wear a little more makeup and maybe do something different with her hair. Kate was attempting unsuccessfully to tune her out when someone came around the corner and stopped to look at the poster Kate was trying to center between the debate club announcements and the flyer for the upcoming jazz band concert.

"Masquerade ball, huh?" said a boy's voice.

Kate looked over her shoulder and almost dropped the poster. Scott Coogan was standing behind her, watching her try to pull a piece of tape off her cheek, where it had gotten stuck. She was so shocked she couldn't respond. All she could do was look at Scott dumbly, like a deer caught in car headlights.

"Sounds like a lot of fun," Scott continued, seeming not to notice her silence. "What are you going to go as?"

"Well, I was thinking of going as Titania, queen of the fairies," Sherrie said, giving Scott one of her prettiest smiles. "How do you think I'd look in a pair of wings?"

Does she have to flirt with everyone? Kate thought as she tried to concentrate on sticking the poster to the wall and not looking at Scott. She'd been waiting all day for him to appear, and now that he had she wasn't at all sure she knew what to do.

"Fine, I guess," Scott said, barely glancing at Sherrie. "What about you, Kate?" He turned back to her. "What are you going to go as?"

Kate turned around. Still trying not to look at Scott, she fumbled for an answer. "I . . . um . . . I . . ." she said.

"Kate doesn't know yet," Sherrie said, moving in between Scott and Kate. "She doesn't have a date or anything."

Kate wanted to kill Sherrie. She didn't know if Sherrie had thrown in the part about Kate's not having a date as a suggestion to Scott or to make him think she wasn't popular enough to be asked. But Scott ignored Sherrie, looking over her shoulder at Kate. He smiled, and Kate smiled back awkwardly, feeling like a little kid as she stared into his eyes. "Is that right?" he asked, moving closer.

Kate nodded, looking up at him. Scott was even more handsome in person than he was in her fantasies. He was taller than she was by a good six inches, and his broad shoulders and wide chest filled out his shirt nicely. *He even smells wonderful*, Kate thought.

"You're taking Terri Fletcher, aren't you?" Sherrie said to Scott, spoiling the moment completely.

Kate's heart sank into her stomach. She remembered the way Scott had looked at Terri in the library, and how they had been laughing at some private joke when she ran out. She thought about how she had wrapped the ribbon around the Ken doll, imagining it was Scott she was tying her heart to. Suddenly she felt like a total fool.

Scott shrugged. Then he looked right at Kate. "We were talking about maybe going, but I don't think that's going to work out. *You* don't want to go with me, do you?"

"Me?" she squeaked.

Scott nodded. "You know, if you're really not going with anyone."

Sherrie turned and looked at Kate, her eyes wide. Kate had never seen her friend at a loss for words before, and she almost started laughing at the expression on Sherrie's face. But Scott was waiting for her answer, and she had to try to remain calm, even if she really felt like screaming and dancing around the hallway. The spell had worked after all! Scott Coogan was actually asking *her* to the dance.

"Well, I hadn't really thought about it," Kate said, trying to sound relaxed.

Sherrie's eyes got even wider, and her mouth dropped open. She spun around. "She means yes," she said. "Yes, she'll go to the dance with you."

"Is that right, Kate?" Scott asked, smiling lazily.

Kate smiled back. "Sure," she said. "I'd love to go with you."

"Great. It's a date. I'll call you later to figure out what we should go as, okay? I'm not so great with that kind of thing, so maybe you'll have some ideas."

Kate nodded, biting her lip to keep from saying anything dumb. Scott turned and walked away, and Kate stared at his retreating back, still partly in shock over what had just occurred. As soon as he was out of sight, Sherrie grabbed Kate's hands.

"I take back everything I ever said," she gushed. "How did you *do* that?"

"Do what?" asked Kate dreamily.

"Do what?" mimicked Sherrie. "Only land the hottest guy in school as your date to the most romantic dance of the year."

"Oh, that," said Kate. "Just lucky, I guess." She found herself thoroughly enjoying Sherrie's shock and bewilderment.

"Wait until the girls hear this," said Sherrie. "They are going to die."

She grabbed Kate's arm and dragged her down the hall in search of Jessica and Tara. Kate couldn't wait to see the expression on her friends' faces when they found out that she was going to the Valentine's Day dance with Scott. But almost as important, she now knew for certain that the spell had worked after all. The magic was real.

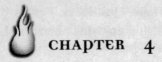

CHAPTER 4

I can't believe it all worked out so perfectly, Kate thought to herself as she lay on her bed later that night thinking about everything that had happened. Jessica and Tara had been shocked at the news of Kate's date. At first they'd insisted that she was playing a joke on them. But Sherrie, after adding a few flourishes to the effect that, really, it had been all her doing, managed to convince them. And if they still didn't totally believe it, all of their doubts were erased when Scott stopped by their table during lunch to say hello to Kate.

Of course, there had been the little problem of having every other boy in school still interested in her. She hadn't figured out what that was all about yet. No fewer than seven different guys had asked her to the dance. Some of them, like Scott, had never even seemed to know she existed before Thursday morning, but suddenly she was the It girl of Beecher Falls High. It was a nice feeling, but a little weird. Kate assumed that her spell had just been too strong.

Maybe I have more power than I thought I did, she thought. Although she had been skeptical about the whole witchcraft thing when she first started reading about it, now that her first spell had worked more or less the way she'd wanted it to, she wondered what else she might be able to do. As an experiment, she pointed her finger at the telephone and willed Scott to call her.

When the phone rang, she jumped and let out a little yelp of surprise. She stared at the phone for a moment as it rang two more times, afraid to pick it up. Then, remembering that it might be Scott, she grabbed it.

"Hello?"

"Hi," said a girl's voice. It was Tara.

"Oh, hi," said Kate.

"Don't sound so thrilled," Tara said sarcastically. "Who did you think it was, Regis phoning because a friend needs your help with the million-dollar question?"

"I thought you might be Scott," Kate admitted.

Tara sighed. "One request for a date and already you're sitting by the phone," she said. "I thought you were a liberated woman."

Kate laughed. "He just said he might call, that's all," she said.

"Maybe he will," said Tara. "In the meantime, have you studied for the chem midterm tomorrow?"

Kate groaned. "I forgot all about it," she admitted. "Not that studying would help any. I'm hopeless when it comes to that stuff."

"Well, I need to pass," said Tara. "I'm going to cram for a couple of hours. If you want to come over, I could use some help."

"Maybe," Kate said. "I have some stuff I need to do here first. I'll call you back in a little bit and let you know, okay?"

She hung up, and almost immediately the phone rang again.

"If you're ordering pizza, I want extra anchovies," she said after picking it up, assuming it was Tara calling back to try to bribe her with food, as she usually did.

"Well, I'm an extra cheese man myself, but I'm willing to change," said a male voice.

"Scott?" said Kate. She felt her face instantly redden. "Sorry. I thought you were Tara. We have this running joke about pizza with anchovies because once we ordered it by mistake and . . . oh, never mind."

Scott laughed. "Don't worry about it," he said. "I think it's cute."

Kate blushed again. *He thinks I'm cute.*

"I was just calling to see if you had any ideas about costumes for the dance," Scott said. "I'm not real good with creative stuff, so I need all the help I can get."

Kate settled back against the pillows on her bed. Now that they were talking, she was starting to relax a little bit. Part of her still couldn't believe that she was talking to Scott Coogan about going on an actual date. She thought hard about what kind of costumes they could wear.

"Do we want funny or serious?" she asked. "I mean, we could go as Winnie the Pooh and Piglet, or we could go as Bonnie and Clyde. What kind of mood are we going for?"

"Well, it *is* Valentine's Day and all," Scott answered. "I was thinking maybe something romantic."

Kate pumped her fist in the air and kicked her feet against the bed. Scott wanted to be romantic! A day before he had never even spoken to her, and now he was talking about her as if they were a couple. Well, practically a couple. And she had witchcraft to thank for it. She thought about Sherrie's saying that it would take a fairy godmother with a magic wand to get Scott to ask her out. It had been more true than Sherrie would ever know, and it gave Kate an idea.

"I know," she said. "We could go as Princess Aurora and Prince Phillip from the Disney version of *Sleeping Beauty*. That's definitely romantic, and it wouldn't be too much work."

"Sounds good to me," Scott said. "What should I wear?"

"I think he wears some kind of nondescript medieval outfit," Kate said. "I'm sure we can find a picture somewhere online."

"I'll get on it," Scott said.

Kate tried to picture Sherrie's face when she saw her and Scott the night of the dance. Since the gym would be decorated like the ballroom in Sleeping Beauty's castle, it would be as if the whole dance had been created just for her and Scott. They'd be the center of attention. She couldn't imagine anything more perfect.

"I'm really looking forward to this," she said. "To tell the truth, I was a little surprised that you asked me."

Scott paused. "I was sort of surprised myself," he admitted. "I mean, everyone kind of expected me to go with Terri. But then last night I found myself thinking about going with you, and the more I thought about it the more I realized that you were the one I really wanted to be there with."

Last night, thought Kate. *Right when I did the spell.* Never mind the forty-eight-hour time frame given in the book. Now there was no doubt in her mind that it was magic that had brought her and Scott together.

"Well, I'm glad you asked me," Kate said.

She and Scott talked for a while about school and football and what they both liked to do for fun. When Kate finally hung up, reluctantly, she was happier than she'd ever been. She wasn't sure she could call Scott her boyfriend, but it looked as if things were definitely heading in that direction.

The phone rang a third time, and she picked it up. "Hello?" she said dreamily, still thinking of Scott.

"Thanks for calling back," Tara said. She sounded angry. "I kept trying to call you, but nobody was picking up call waiting."

"Sorry," said Kate. "Scott called. Do you still want me to come over?"

"Don't bother," Tara said. "It's too late now anyway. I'll finish up by myself."

She hung up. Kate put the phone down. Why did Tara have to ruin her perfect evening? Kate didn't see what the big deal was about a little studying. It wasn't like either of them was going to do well on the test anyway. It would take a miracle for them to get good grades.

Or magic, said a voice in Kate's head.

She thought about it for a minute. Magic *had* gotten her a date with Scott. Could it also help her get good grades? It seemed a little greedy to be doing another spell so quickly. Then again, she *did* need help. It was late, and she hadn't even cracked her chem stuff. Maybe a little boost wouldn't be asking too much.

She picked up the spell book and looked through it. Sure enough, toward the back she found a spell for helping the caster excel when tested. "This spell will help someone remember information learned in preparation for an exam," she read. Plus, the disclaimer at the bottom didn't say anything about a delay in the effects. Well, she hadn't exactly learned anything to remember yet, but maybe it would work anyway. After all, she hadn't followed the Come to Me Love Spell exactly the way it was written, and the effects had been even stronger than planned. This one would undoubtedly work for her.

Ten minutes later she was sitting in a circle of candles with both the spell book and her chemistry textbook in her lap. The spell book told her to close her eyes and picture herself doing well on her exam. She imagined herself in Miss Blackwood's classroom. She saw the periodic table hanging on the front wall. She imagined herself looking at her test paper and filling in the answers easily. Then she envisioned herself going through the steps of the lab practical, measuring things into beakers and writing down the results.

When she had a good image of all these things being done successfully, she opened her eyes and, holding the chemistry textbook tightly in her hands, read the words of the spell.

> *Facts and figures, rules and laws,*
> *fill my mind and give me cause*
> *to answer questions, fulfill tasks,*
> *and know the things I shall be asked.*
> *When I'm challenged, give me aid,*
> *to receive a passing grade.*
> *All this knowledge stay with me.*
> *As I will, so mote it be.*

I don't feel any smarter, she thought as she sat there, waiting for something to happen. She tried going over some familiar chemistry formulas in her head. Nothing came to her. But maybe the spell needed time to work. The love spell had taken a little while to get going. It would probably take this one some time, too. She decided the best thing to do was to just wait.

Extinguishing the candles, she returned them to the box. The Ken doll was still in there as well. She took it out, held it in front of her, and kissed it, immediately feeling foolish. She thought about what it would be like to kiss Scott. She was sure he would kiss her at the dance. It would be exactly like the Sleeping Beauty fairy tale come true. She put the doll back into the box, and hid the box in her closet again.

She still wasn't sure what to do about the chemistry test. The book didn't say exactly how the spell worked, but it *did* say that it was meant to help her remember things. There wasn't time to read all the material that would be on the midterm, though, so she would have to hope things would work out. Just in case it would help, she decided to sleep with her chemistry textbook and notebook under her pillow, hoping maybe the spell would help some of the information stick in her head. It sounded weird, but weirder things had already happened to her.

Kate woke up the next morning with a cramp in her neck from sleeping all night with her head on the chemistry book. As she rubbed the sore muscles with her fingers, she knew she'd made a horrible mistake. She was suddenly very much aware that she was about to walk into a midterm exam for a subject she knew very little about. She didn't seem to know anything more about chemistry than she had the night before.

Brushing thoughts of the exam from her mind, she showered and dressed. Instead of wearing her usual outfit of jeans and a shirt, she decided to wear something with a little more style, just in case Scott wanted to hang out with her. Pulling on a long black skirt and a form-fitting V-neck sweater, Kate imagined Scott checking her out and liking what he saw. Thinking about him made her feel better, and by the time she left for school she'd forgotten about the exam.

Sherrie, Jessica, and Tara were hanging out by the lockers when Kate got to school. Sizing up her outfit, they looked at her with raised eyebrows.

"Dressing up for your new man?" Sherrie asked. Her voice was pleasant, but Kate thought there was more than a hint of sarcasm in her statement.

"Just trying to keep up with you," she answered just as sweetly as she put her stuff in her locker. Then she turned to Tara.

"I'm really sorry about last night," she said.

Tara looked away from her. "I said it was okay," she said, but she didn't sound like she'd forgiven Kate at all.

"What's up with you guys today?" Kate asked,

trying to sound upbeat. "Did someone die?"

None of them said anything, but Kate caught Jessica and Sherrie exchanging a look.

"What?" she said. "What's going on?"

"You should probably know that people have been talking," Sherrie said finally.

"Talking?" said Kate. "About what?"

"About you," said Jess, as if breaking bad news.

"What about me?" asked Kate.

Her friends looked at each other again. Clearly, they knew something they didn't want her to know. Finally, Jessica sighed.

"You weren't the first girl Scott Coogan asked to the dance," she said. Then she looked at Sherrie and Tara before adding, "He asked Terri Fletcher."

"What are you talking about?" Kate said. "He told me that he had been thinking of asking Terri but that he didn't."

"That's a boy for you," Sherrie said, butting in. "He did ask Terri. On Wednesday. Then he called her the next day and told her he didn't want to go with her."

"How do you know this?" Kate asked faintly. There was a sick feeling growing in her stomach.

"*Everybody* knows it," Sherrie said, and Kate couldn't help but notice that her friend seemed a little pleased with herself.

Kate didn't know what to say. She felt as if she was being attacked. "I can't help it if Scott asked me and not Terri," she said.

"Maybe not," Sherrie said. "But Terri thinks you set out to get him. And she's not the only one."

"What are you saying?" Kate demanded. "Do you think I did it on purpose?" She looked from Sherrie to Jessica to Tara.

Jessica shrugged. "I don't know," she said. "It does seem strange that a guy who never noticed you before suddenly asks you out and dumps the girl he asked in the first place."

Kate looked at Tara. "And what do you think?" she asked. She knew she sounded really angry, but she couldn't help it.

"I don't think it's your fault," she said carefully. "But I also don't think it's like you to stand one of your friends up to talk to a guy, and you did that last night."

Kate didn't know what to say. She felt like she was on trial. And to make things worse, her very best friends were the ones judging her.

"I've known you guys since we were all six years old," Kate said. "I can't believe you would listen to what other people are saying about me!"

"We're not saying you did anything wrong," Sherrie reassured her. "We're just saying you should be careful. You don't want people to think the wrong thing."

Kate looked away. "I think they already do," she said. "I've got to go."

Hugging her books to her chest, she walked away as quickly as she could without running. Part of her hoped that her friends would come after her, but another part wanted to get away from them. How dare they accuse her of doing something to win Scott away from Terri? It wasn't her fault that he had asked her out and then changed his mind.

Or was it? Had the spell really done that? Did magic work that way? She hadn't meant to hurt anyone's feelings. She'd just wanted Scott to like her.

As she walked to class, she couldn't help but notice that some people were watching her. Most of them were boys. She was getting used to that. But now some of the girls were staring as she passed them as well. She thought she heard some of them whisper as she went by, but she didn't want to know what they were saying, so she kept going until she reached the chemistry room. She went to her seat and sat down, pretending to look at her notebook as the other students filed in. Tara came in and took the seat next to Kate, but Kate didn't say anything.

"All right," said Miss Blackwood, entering the room as the bell rang and closing the door behind her. "The midterm will have two parts. The first part consists of twenty-five questions. The second is a short experiment. I'll give you the instructions for the lab when you've completed the first part of the test. You have the entire period, so take your time."

She walked around the class handing out test papers. When Kate received hers, she turned it over and read through the questions. Her heart sank. She hadn't studied most of the material on the test. She didn't even know what some of the terms meant.

As she looked at the questions, however, words and formulas began to form in her mind. Sometimes they were sort of familiar, but more often she had almost no idea what they meant. She wasn't sure if she really knew anything or whether she just thought she did because of the spell, but she didn't have anything to lose. She quickly filled in the blanks for the first three questions and moved on. Her pencil practically flew over the paper as she read the questions and waited for the answers to come to her. While the students around her sat looking stupidly at their tests, Kate worked rapidly. She wasn't sure that what she was writing down was right, but it all seemed to make sense in a way she couldn't exactly explain.

When she finished with the first part of the test, she walked up to Miss Blackwood's desk. Everyone in the class watched her as she handed in her paper.

"You're not finished, are you?" her teacher asked.

Kate nodded.

Miss Blackwood gave her a peculiar look. "All right," she said. "Here are the instructions for the lab."

Kate took the instructions and walked to the back of the room. She felt people watching her, but she tried to ignore them. She wanted to concentrate on her lab work.

The equipment for the experiments was already set up, and Kate got right to work. Again, she didn't entirely understand the purpose of the experiment, but she seemed to know exactly what she needed to do. She quickly became engrossed in watching the liquid in her test tubes, and she barely noticed when the other students started coming back one by one and beginning their labs. She was busy taking measurements and recording her results.

The time seemed to fly by, and Kate was surprised to see that when she was finished there were still fifteen minutes left in the class period. As she cleaned up her equipment and prepared to hand in her results to Miss Blackwood, she noticed that Tara, who was using a table near hers, was barely halfway through her experiment. Not only that, but Kate could see that Tara had botched her work pretty badly. Kate felt sorry for her friend—until she remembered their encounter earlier in the morning.

"I thought you said you didn't study," Tara whispered as Kate passed by on her way to the sink.

"I didn't much," said Kate. "I guess I just studied the right things."

Tara sniffed. "You seem to be doing everything right these days."

Kate ignored the comment and, snatching up her paper, walked to the front of the room and placed the paper on Miss Blackwood's desk. The teacher looked surprised, but Kate left the room before she could say anything. She wasn't in the mood for talking.

As she approached her locker she saw that Scott was standing there, and she knew he was waiting for her. When he saw her, he smiled and waved, and suddenly all of the bad feelings that had been weighing her down disappeared. Who cared if people were talking about her? Who cared if her friends were acting strangely? Scott Coogan was waiting to talk to her. And she was feeling better and better about the chemistry test. She was getting everything she'd ever wanted with the help of the spells.

Besides, it was Friday. She just had to make it through one day, and then it would be the weekend. She knew that by Monday the whole Terri scandal would have blown over and things would be back to normal. She just had to wait it out.

CHAPTER 5

But first Kate had to survive the rest of Friday, and it was hard. The story about Scott's ditching Terri and asking Kate out had spread like wildfire, and Kate couldn't help thinking that Sherrie had had something to do with how quickly the word got around. However it had happened, though, people were most definitely talking about her. And anyone who didn't know about it did after Scott walked Kate to her second period class, holding her hand. Again, Kate felt the peculiar mix of elation and worry as she walked beside him, her fingers entwined with his. Everything was happening so fast, and the fact that she had made it all happen made her feel a little invincible.

Even though she adored what was happening with Scott, she wasn't totally happy. Boys were still paying attention to her, but it was becoming distracting. She had thought that when people knew she was going to the dance with Scott they would quit leering at her, so she couldn't understand why it was still going on now that she had what she wanted.

Even worse, things between her and her friends were still strained. At lunch she sat with Scott and his friends. She enjoyed the fact that the other students were looking at them, and she loved being included in the conversation. But it felt strange to not be sitting with her friends. She couldn't remember the last time they hadn't sat at the same table to eat lunch. To make things even harder, the one time she looked over at them, Sherrie shot her a nasty look and said something to Tara and Jessica that made them laugh. Kate knew that they were laughing at her, and she tried to not care. After all, they had practically accused her of doing something wrong. Still, it felt strange to not have them around her, joking and talking about what they were going to do over the weekend.

The weekend was the hardest part. While part of her really wanted to hang out with Sherrie, Tara, and Jessica, she thought it was best if they had some time apart. But she didn't know how she was going to explain to her parents that she wasn't hanging out with her friends over the weekend. They normally did everything together, and it was going to look weird if she stayed home alone. As she walked home, she tried to come up with a plausible explanation. To her relief, when she arrived at the house she discovered that Kyle had made a surprise weekend visit home from college.

That made things a little easier—it meant that the family spent the weekend going out to eat and seeing movies, and her parents were too busy asking Kyle how things were at college to get around to asking her anything. On Sunday morning they went to church, and when Kyle left on Sunday afternoon Kate worked on her history paper. Now that she knew a little bit about what witchcraft could do, she was finding the research more interesting. And when the phone rang on Sunday night and it was Scott calling to talk for a little while, it almost made the fact that her friends were giving her the silent treatment okay.

But now it was Monday. Kate hadn't spoken to her friends since Friday, and she wasn't sure what kind of reception to expect when she walked into school. She was almost relieved when she didn't see them standing around the lockers, as they usually were. But a few minutes later she heard Sherrie's unmistakable voice.

"That dress is so cute on you, Jess. It's definitely better than the green one."

Kate turned around. Jessica, Tara, and Sherrie were standing there, all of them in new outfits.

"Hey, guys," Kate said tentatively. "Great clothes."

"We had a little shopping spree this weekend," Jessica said. "You know—girls' day out."

Kate felt a stab of jealousy. They'd gone out together, and they hadn't even invited her, hadn't even given her the chance to say she was busy with her family. But at least they were talking to her again. That was something.

"Sorry you couldn't come," Sherrie said, as if reading Kate's thoughts. "But we figured you'd be busy with other . . . commitments."

"Well, Kyle came home for the weekend," Kate said. She knew Sherrie had a thing for her brother and that she would be annoyed that she hadn't had a chance to come over and drool over him. Still, it didn't make her feel much better about being left out. Before all this Scott business, they would have gone out together and had a good time. She felt as if she was being punished.

"We'll all go next time," Jessica said, trying to sound positive. "We have to shop for our dance costumes pretty soon."

"Sure," Kate said, but she felt anything but confident.

Sherrie and Jessica left for their class, and Kate walked to chemistry with Tara.

"She's still mad, isn't she?" Kate asked, meaning Sherrie. Kate, Tara, and Jessica sometimes had misunderstandings, and even fights, but it was Sherrie who was the undisputed champ of grudge holding.

"You know Sherrie," Tara answered. "She always has to be the center of attention. Give her a few days. She'll settle down."

They walked into Miss Blackwood's room and took their seats. The mood in the class was subdued, because everyone knew that they'd be getting the results of their midterms back. When Miss Blackwood came in carrying a stack of test papers, they all held their breath.

"Well," their teacher said, "I've graded all of your papers."

No one said a word as they waited for her to continue. Miss Blackwood picked up the test on the top of the pile.

"I have to say, I was a little surprised by the results," she said. "The grades were better than I had expected."

There was a collective sigh from the students, and some even smiled.

"At least *some* of the grades were better than I expected," Miss Blackwood said, dropping the test paper back onto the stack. The sighs of relief turned into groans.

Miss Blackwood walked down the rows of desks, holding the tests in her hands. She stopped in front of one student and paused.

"As usual, we had an A," she said. She took a paper and handed it to Annie Crandall, who smiled slightly and immediately stuck the paper into her notebook without looking at it.

Annie's getting an A was no surprise at all. She always got A's in chemistry. In fact, she was so far ahead of everyone else that Miss Blackwood didn't count her score when setting the grading curve for everyone else.

Miss Blackwood continued walking. "However, we also had another A," she said.

Everyone looked around, trying to figure out who might have done so well on one of Miss Blackwood's tests. As she moved down the rows, they waited for her to stop and present the lucky person with the paper.

Miss Blackwood stopped in front of Kate and held out her test. "Congratulations, Miss Morgan," she said. "You scored a ninety-seven, the highest grade in the class after Miss Crandall's."

Kate looked at the bright red number circled at the top of her test paper. It had an exclamation point beside it, and with good reason. She could hardly believe it herself. She'd thought she'd done well, but this was better than she could ever have imagined. The highest score she'd ever gotten on one of Miss Blackwood's tests before was a 78.

"I think Miss Morgan's score proves that this material is not as difficult as some of the other test scores would suggest," Miss Blackwood said as she began to pass out the other test papers. "I'm disappointed that so few of you improved from the last test to this one, as she did."

Tara was handed her paper, and Kate looked at it. She'd gotten a 69.

"I passed," Tara said with a sigh. "Barely, but I passed." She smiled at Kate, and it was the first genuine smile she'd given her since their mis-understanding the week before.

"Normally I would consider a grade of sixty-five passing on an exam such as this one," Miss Blackwood said as she gave the last couple of tests back. "But given Miss Morgan's grade, I can only assume that the rest of you should be capable of the same results. Therefore, the passing grade on this exam is seventy."

There were exclamations of protest from a number of students.

"That's not fair," said Robert Pela, who waved his test with a 65 on it in the air. "I studied really hard for this."

"Not as hard as Miss Morgan did, apparently," said Miss Blackwood. "I'm sorry, but I have to set the curve according to the highest grade. Perhaps next time you'll all put as much effort into learning the material as Kate did."

Robert turned and glared at Kate. So did a number of other students. Suddenly, her 97 turned from a badge of honor to a mark of shame. She looked over at Tara, hoping she at least would be happy for her. Instead, her friend looked like she was about to start crying.

"What's wrong?" Kate asked.

"What's wrong?" Tara said quietly so that Miss Blackwood wouldn't hear. "Don't you get it? I failed the exam. That means I have a failing grade in the class. I'm going to be on academic probation, which means I can't play in any games for the next two weeks."

Kate had forgotten about Tara's academic troubles. She wasn't the best student, and she was having a really hard time this year. Her grades in math and chemistry were borderline failing, and she'd been told that unless she improved them she would have to sit out two weeks' worth of games. The chemistry midterm had been her last hope, and now she'd failed.

"I studied so hard!" Tara wailed. "And I would have passed . . ."

"If it weren't for me," Kate said, finishing her sentence.

Tara looked at her and didn't say anything.

"I'm really sorry," Kate said. "I didn't mean to do it."

"I even asked you to study with me," Tara said quietly.

"I said I was sorry," Kate tried again.

Tara didn't say anything, but Kate knew she had done something awful. For the rest of the class, she sat staring at her test paper. The spell she'd done had given her a good grade, all right, but she had made a lot of other people fail in the process. Was it worth it? If things were supposed to be working out the way she wanted, why did she feel so terrible?

After class Tara left without waiting for Kate. But several other people made sure they spoke to her, and what they had to say wasn't particularly nice.

"Thanks a lot," Robert said as he passed her on the way out. "Next time you plan on ruining the curve, make sure you let us in on it."

"Way to go," said another girl, and Kate knew it wasn't a compliment.

"I got a failing grade thanks to you," said Alan Folger. "But I'll forgive you if you go out with me this weekend."

Kate ignored him and brushed past the other students waiting to insult her, and made her getaway. She was beginning to feel like there was no place in the school she could go where someone wasn't angry with her. Even the sight of Scott walking toward her didn't cheer her up.

"Hey," he said. "What's wrong? You look upset."

"I aced my chem test," she said.

"And that's a problem?" Scott asked. "I've never dated anyone who was mad about being smart."

Scott put his arm around her and steered her down the hall. Having him next to her, Kate felt a little better. She felt protected and safe. With Scott there, it didn't matter if people were angry at her. She *was* proud of having done well on the test. It wasn't her fault the other students hadn't done well. It wasn't her fault that she was able to make a spell work.

By the time she and Scott reached the end of the

hall, she felt a lot better. When he said good-bye and went into his next class, she walked to her own class thinking that things would be okay after all. Her friends couldn't stay mad at her forever, and people would eventually forget about the test. She did feel bad that Tara would have to miss out on basketball for two weeks, but she would find some way to make it up to her. Maybe she could even do a spell to help out.

She was so busy thinking about all the things that were going on that she wasn't watching where she was going. When she bumped into someone and dropped her books, she barely noticed.

"I'm sorry," she began, picking up her fallen books. "I wasn't looking and—"

"I bet you weren't," a girl said. Kate looked up. Terri Fletcher was standing in front of her. A group of Terri's friends were with her, and they looked at Kate with undisguised hostility.

"You don't seem to care who you run into—or over—do you?" Terri said. "As long as you get what you want."

"Look," said Kate. "I'm sorry I ran into you, but it was an accident."

"I suppose what happened with Scott was an accident, too," Terri said.

Kate looked into Terri's angry face. The older girl was taller than she was, and Kate didn't want any kind of confrontation.

"I'm sorry Scott changed his m-mind about

going to the d-dance with you," Kate stammered. "But it's not my fault."

"Oh, yeah?" said another girl, behind Terri. "And I suppose it isn't your fault that my boyfriend keeps asking me why I can't be more like you."

"I don't even know who your boyfriend is," Kate said.

The girl laughed. "Little Miss Innocent. Right. Look, I don't know what you think you're up to, but we've had just about enough of it."

Kate looked around at the girls. They seemed to be circling her, and she felt trapped. *They're like the mobs that burned the witches*, Kate thought suddenly. They were angry, and she was the person they were angry at.

"But I didn't *do* anything!" Kate said. She knew she was going to cry if they kept it up, and she didn't want to do that.

"I saw you talking to my boyfriend," another girl said. She stood in front of Kate, her eyes flashing. "It was obvious you were flirting with him."

"He was talking to *me*," Kate said helplessly. "I can't stop people from talking to me."

The girl put her finger in front of Kate's face. "You just stay away from what doesn't belong to you, got it?"

Kate felt the circle of girls closing in on her. Her heart was racing, and her mouth was dry. She wanted to tell them she was innocent of all the things they were accusing her of, but she couldn't.

She knew that no matter what she said, they wouldn't believe her.

"I don't know what you *did* to make Scott change his mind," Terri said, emphasizing the word, "but don't think he's going to be with you for long. Once he sees what kind of girl you are, he'll drop you so fast you won't know what to do."

Kate felt the first tears forming in her eyes, and she tried to hold them back. She'd never felt so awful in her life. All she wanted to do was run away and hide, to be somewhere where people weren't yelling at her.

"In the meantime, try to keep your hands off everyone else," a girl said.

Kate couldn't take any more. Rushing forward, she pushed her way through the crowd of girls and ran down the stairs. She could hear them laughing at her as she stumbled and almost fell, her books scattering on the steps. She grabbed them and fled, just wanting to get away from the cruel voices.

The tears she'd been holding back came out now, flowing hot and wet down her cheeks as she started to sob. Everything was going wrong, and she didn't know how to stop it. She'd just wanted to be happy. Why was everything out of control?

She ran until she came to the library. Classes had started, and she had no intention of going into her math class looking the way she did. The library looked deserted, so she pushed open the doors and went inside. She walked to the end of the rows of books and turned into the aisle between two shelves. Slumping to the floor, she put her head in her hands and cried.

Her whole body shook as all of the anxiety and unhappiness poured out of her. Her life was a mess, and she didn't know what she could do to fix it. She couldn't help it that all of the boys were paying attention to her. She couldn't help it if her good grade had ruined things for the rest of the class. She couldn't help it if Scott wanted to take her to the Valentine's Day dance. So why did she feel like she was being punished for doing something wrong?

She wiped her eyes and looked around. She noticed that she happened to be sitting in the row of books where she'd found the book of spells.

I wish I'd never seen that book, she thought. *That's what caused all these problems in the first place.*

She knew it was the spells she'd done that were making things go wrong. But she didn't know why they weren't working correctly. She'd done everything the way the book said to. Well, mostly the way the book said to. She had to admit that she'd improvised a little bit. Still, she didn't think she'd done anything to make things turn out as badly as they had.

She wished she knew someone else who knew something about magic. If only she had someone she could talk to about what was going on, things would be better. Her friends were definitely out.

They probably weren't even speaking to her. She couldn't talk to her parents. They would think she was nuts. There was nobody.

Maybe there is, she thought. After all, she had checked the book out. Maybe someone else had checked it out at some point, too. And maybe that person had done some of the spells. If she could find out who it was, she might be able to get some help figuring out where she'd gone wrong. But how could she find out who else had checked the book out?

She had an idea. Standing up, she straightened her clothes and fixed her hair. She hoped her crying hadn't made her look too awful. Her plan depended upon her looking totally normal. She took a few deep breaths, then walked up to the circulation desk and smiled at the librarian behind the counter. She was relieved it wasn't a student worker, who probably would have been someone who was mad at her for one reason or another.

"Can I help you?" the woman asked.

"I hope so," Kate said. "I checked out a book last week for one of my classes, and I found a personal letter in it. But without a name," she added quickly, trying not to think about how much sense she wasn't making. "I think whoever checked it out before I did must have left it in there as a bookmark or something, and I wanted to return it."

"Well, that's very thoughtful of you," the librarian said. "Most people probably wouldn't have bothered."

"I know I wouldn't want to lose a piece of personal correspondence," Kate said innocently. "Is there any way for you to tell me who signed the book out last?"

"What's the title of the book?" the woman asked.

Kate told her, trying not to sound self-conscious about having checked out a book of spells. But if the librarian thought it was strange, she didn't let on. She turned to the file of circulation cards and pulled open a drawer. Flipping through them, she paused and pulled one out. She turned back to Kate and held it out to her.

"There you go," she said.

Kate took the card and looked at it. The most recent name on the card was her own. Above it there was another one. In fact, the same name was written on the seven lines above Kate's. The same person had checked the book out repeatedly.

And that person was Annie Crandall.

CHAPTER 6

Kate stared at the circulation card. Annie Crandall? She couldn't believe it. No-nonsense Annie, who lived for science, had repeatedly checked out a book about witchcraft. Why? Kate looked at the name again, wondering if perhaps she'd read it incorrectly. But there it was, written seven times in the librarian's precise handwriting. Annie Crandall had checked the book out for almost two months straight.

Kate realized that the librarian was staring at her. She handed the card back and smiled.

"Thanks a lot," she said. "I'll make sure that girl gets her letter back."

The librarian returned the card to the circulation file, and Kate walked away. She was still having a hard time accepting the fact that Annie had been reading the book. Annie seemed like such a logical type. Kate couldn't picture her lighting candles and saying spells. She was just too, well, normal for things like that.

I wonder if that's how she does so well in chemistry, Kate thought as she left the library. It would certainly explain why Annie was always at the top of the class. Kate remembered the look Annie had given her when Miss Blackwood had announced her grade, and she wondered what Annie would say if she knew Kate was using magic, too.

Still, Kate didn't know how she was going to approach Annie for help. She'd never really even spoken to her. She didn't want to just walk up and say, "Hey, tried any spells lately?" If Annie had been reading the book for some other reason, she might think Kate was crazy. Everyone already apparently thought she was up to no good; she didn't need it getting out that she was playing around with witchcraft as well.

But she definitely needed to figure out what was going on, and Annie seemed to be the only person who might be able to help her. She checked her watch and saw that her next class would be starting in a few minutes.

Kate thought through the rest of her day. She had art and English next. Annie wasn't in either of those classes, so the earliest Kate might run into her would be at lunch. She tried to remember whether or not she and Annie had the same lunch period. She couldn't remember ever having seen her in the cafeteria. Then again, she thought, she'd never looked for her before.

She tried to keep a low profile for her next two

classes. For one thing, she didn't want to run into Terri Fletcher or any of her friends. Besides, she could tell by the way that people shot glances at her in the halls that she was still public enemy number one among a good portion of the student body.

Worst of all, she had to avoid Scott. She knew things would get even worse if people saw them together, at least for the moment, so she tried to stay away from him. After art, when she saw him walking down the hall toward her, she ducked down the stairs before he could catch up. And she almost ran into him again outside her English class, where he'd gone to look for her, but she managed to hide in the girls' room until he had to leave for his own class. She knew he would be confused about her behavior, but she couldn't risk causing a scene. Not until she sorted out a few things.

After English class was over, she raced to the cafeteria. Scott would be there shortly, as would her friends, and she didn't want to run into any of them. She just wanted to find Annie. But as she scanned the tables and the food service line, she didn't see her anywhere. She was just about to give up and go spend the period in the library when she noticed someone tucked into a corner of the cafeteria. Her back was to Kate, but Kate recognized the single long braid that fell down the girl's back. It was Annie. She was all alone, and there was a book open in front of her. Before she could lose her nerve, Kate walked over to the table.

"Hi," she said, not sure of how to proceed.

Annie looked up. She was eating an apple and had just taken a bite. She looked at Kate and then looked around with a confused expression.

"Are you talking to me?" she asked doubtfully.

Kate nodded. "Yeah," she said, suddenly incredibly nervous. "I'm . . . um . . . Kate."

"I know who you are," Annie said. She didn't sound either pleased or annoyed.

"I guess you do," Kate said nervously. "Look, I know we don't know each other very well—"

"We don't know each other at all," Annie said, interrupting.

Kate paused. "No, I guess we don't," she said. "Not technically, anyway." She stopped, unsure of what to say next.

Annie took another bite of her apple and munched on it. She stared at Kate, waiting for her to say something. When Kate didn't, Annie looked away. "I guess I should get back to my book," she said.

"Book," Kate said, suddenly remembering why she had come to talk to Annie in the first place. "That's what it was. I want to talk to you about a book."

Annie looked up. "A book?" she said. "You want to talk to me about a book?"

Kate looked around. The cafeteria was filling up. Already some of Scott's friends had settled into their usual table, and she knew that he would be coming in soon. A few tables away, she saw some of the girls who had confronted her earlier watching her. One of them, the one who had stuck her finger in Kate's face, said something to another girl and they all laughed meanly. Kate felt her face flush with embarrassment.

"Are you okay?" Annie asked her. "You look kind of sick."

Kate sat down in the chair next to Annie. "I'm okay," she said. "Well, I'm not okay, but I'm not sick. I just have a problem. One I think you might be able to help me with."

"Me?" said Annie. "What can I do?"

"You checked a book out of the library," Kate said.

Annie shrugged. "I check a lot of books out of the library," she said. "So what?"

"Well, you checked this one out seven times in a row," Kate continued.

An uneasy look passed over Annie's face for a moment and she looked away. When she looked back, she seemed fine again. "Seven times?" she said. "I don't remember doing that."

"Well, you did," Kate said. Then she brought her voice down to a whisper. "The book is called *Spells and Charms for the Modern Witch.* Does that sound familiar?"

Annie put her apple core into her lunch bag and rolled up the bag. "I don't really remember," she said. "Maybe I did. Maybe I needed it for a class or something." She started to get up.

Kate grabbed her arm. Annie looked startled.

"For two months straight?" Kate said, looking up at Annie.

Annie glanced around the room. Kate was afraid the other girl was going to run away from her, and she gripped Annie's arm more tightly.

"Please," she said. "I need to know. Did you do anything with that book?"

"Maybe I read it," Annie said. "I don't really remember."

"But did you *try* any of it?" Kate asked.

"I really have to go," Annie said. "I have to study for a test."

"Why not just do a spell?" Kate said. "Isn't that how you get all your other grades?"

Annie glared at Kate as if she'd been slapped.

"Let go of me," she snapped. She jerked her arm out of Kate's grasp and walked away quickly, hugging her books to her chest.

Oh, great, Kate thought. *I just went and insulted the one person who might be able to help me.* Getting up, she walked after Annie, who had disappeared through the cafeteria doors.

When Kate exited the cafeteria, she saw Annie at the end of the hall. Running quickly, she caught up with the retreating girl.

"I'm sorry," she said, walking beside Annie, who refused to look at her. "I don't know who else to ask. Your name was on the checkout card for the book."

Annie stopped and turned to look at Kate. "What do you want?" she said. "And why do you think I can help you just because I checked some stupid book out of the library?"

Annie's face was red, and she almost looked as if she were about to start crying.

"You did try some of the spells, didn't you?" Kate said suddenly. Something about the way Annie was reacting made her sure that she had.

Before Annie could answer, Scott appeared from around the corner. When he saw Kate, he waved and started toward them. "Hey," he called. "I've been looking all over for you."

Kate groaned. "We don't have much time," she said to Annie. "I need your help. If you know anything about the stuff in that book, you've got to tell me."

Scott was getting closer. Annie looked at him, then at Kate. She opened her mouth and closed it again.

"Please," Kate said. "Just tell me."

Annie sighed. "Come to my house after school," she said. "We'll talk. I'm at Thirty-nine Ash Lane."

"The street just past the college library?" Kate asked.

Annie nodded. "Come at three-thirty," she said.

Kate would have to skip basketball practice to go to Annie's house, but she wasn't exactly looking forward to spending an hour and a half with Tara and Jessica right then anyway. She'd make up some excuse for Coach Saliers. She looked into Annie's eyes. "Thanks," she said.

Annie smiled slightly. "Don't thank me yet," she said. "I didn't say there was anything I could do."

She turned and walked away as Scott caught up with them.

"Where have you been all day?" he asked Kate. "It's like you're avoiding me or something."

Kate tried to sound happy to see him, but she was worried that someone might see them. As she and Scott walked down the hall, she kept glancing around for signs of trouble. When Scott reached for her hand, she dropped her books and busied herself picking them up.

"What's gotten into you?" Scott asked as he helped her.

"Nothing," Kate said. "I guess I'm just nervous about the dance and all."

"Nervous?" Scott said. "Don't be nervous." He put his arm around her and continued walking. "The dance is going to be great, especially with you on my arm."

Kate had waited a long time to have Scott say something like that to her. She wanted to enjoy it. But ever since the incident with the other girls, she had felt like all eyes were on her. And sure enough, as she and Scott walked past the cafeteria doors, they swung open and Terri Fletcher walked out with one of her friends. When they saw Scott and Kate, they stopped talking and just stared.

"Hi, Scott," Terri said icily, but Scott didn't seem to notice the tone in her voice.

"Hey," he said. "How's it going?"

Terri's face pinched up. She turned and rushed down the hallway, away from them.

"Nice going," her friend said to Scott. Then, as she passed them, she said so only Kate could hear her, "You'd better watch your step."

"Maybe we shouldn't go to the dance together," Kate said to Scott after the girl was gone. "It seems to be causing a lot of trouble."

Scott hugged her close. "Don't you worry about them," he said. "They're just jealous because you snagged me."

For a moment, Kate felt the warm joy of being with the boy of her dreams flow over her again. Maybe Scott was right. Maybe everything would be all right. Maybe she was just overreacting to things.

"Besides," Scott said, "I have a big surprise for you."

"For me?" Kate said. "What is it?"

Scott grinned. "Not until tomorrow," he said. "But I promise you, it's going to be great."

No matter how hard she begged, Scott wouldn't tell her what his big surprise was. She tried for the rest of the lunch period to get it out of him, but when the bell rang she wasn't any closer to finding out what he had in store for her. Still, just knowing that he was planning something was enough, and for the rest of the day Kate felt almost normal again.

After school, she ran home to change and grab something to eat. Then she headed back out and walked to Annie's house. It wasn't hard to find. The area of town where Kate and Annie lived was centered around the campus of Jasper College. The beautiful old stone buildings of the school, and the wide, tree-lined lawns that surrounded them, formed a big square. The streets all ran parallel to the square, making it easy to walk around. In the fall the streets were filled with students walking or riding their bikes to classes. In winter, they scurried by with their hats pulled over their ears and their scarves wrapped around their necks.

Kate walked until she came to the big college library with its wide steps and students going in and out of the revolving glass doors. At the corner, she turned onto Ash Lane. Number 39 sat at the far end of the street. It was a huge Victorian house painted light green with yellow, dark green, and deep red trim. Although the paint was faded and the house looked lived in, it didn't look run-down. Even in the chill of winter, the garden outside looked neat and orderly. The windows were filled with warm light behind the curtains, and there was a thick stream of smoke coming out of the chimney.

Kate went up the steps and rang the bell. A minute later the door opened and Annie appeared.

"Come on in," she said, sounding almost surprised to see Kate.

Inside, the house was even cozier than the

outside looked. The floors were dark polished wood, and there were carpets everywhere. From the hallway, Kate could see what looked to be lots of rooms opening into one another. They were all painted in rich colors.

"Your house is beautiful," Kate said as Annie took her coat and hung it in a hall closet.

"It's my aunt's house, really," Annie said. "We've lived here since we were little," she said.

"We?" asked Kate.

"My sister and I," Annie explained.

As if on cue, a little girl ran into the hallway. She looked like a miniature version of Annie, with the same long braid hanging down her back.

"I'm Meg," she said to Kate. "I'm nine. How old are you?"

"I'm Kate, and I'm fifteen," Kate said.

The little girl smiled. "The same age as Annie. Are you friends?"

Kate didn't know how to answer that question. She looked at Annie. "I think maybe we are," she said.

"Good," said Meg. "Annie needs friends. That's what Aunt Sarah says."

"Okay," Annie said. "I think it's time for your snack. How about some cookies?"

Meg ran into another room and Annie followed her, with Kate close behind. They went into a big kitchen, where Meg was already taking milk out of the refrigerator.

"Does your friend want some?" she asked.

Annie turned to Kate. "Milk and cookies?" she asked, raising an eyebrow.

"You know, that sounds really good right about now," Kate said.

Meg and Annie busied themselves pouring milk into glasses and putting chocolate chip cookies on plates. Then Annie sent Meg into the other room. "Kate and I are going to go up to my room for a little while," she said. "You can watch TV if you want."

"I'd rather read, if you don't mind," Meg replied. "I'm reading *Alice in Wonderland*," she explained to Kate. "I'm at the part where Alice eats the mushroom and gets really big."

After Meg left, Annie headed for a stairway at the back of the kitchen. Kate followed her. It turned out to be a narrow set of steps that went up a flight and turned a corner before going up some more.

"I feel like we're climbing to the moon," Kate commented as the stairs turned yet again. Her house was also an old Victorian, like most of the houses in the neighborhood around the college, but it was nowhere near as large and rambling as Annie's.

"This was the stairway that kitchen maids used when this place was first built," Annie said as they went up, "so they wouldn't bother anyone when they got up early in the morning. My room is all the way at the top of the house."

"Very convenient for late-night kitchen raids," Kate commented.

They finally reached the top, where Annie opened a door and they stepped through.

"You weren't kidding," said Kate, looking around. They were in a huge room. There were windows on three of the walls, and through them Kate could see the tops of the pine trees outside. "This is like being in a castle or something."

"That's why I like it," Annie said as she set the plate of cookies on a dresser. "And it's quiet."

The enormous room had wooden floors like the rest of the house. Annie's giant brass bed was against one of the walls, which were painted a warm honey color, and there was an equally huge old desk beneath one of the windows. The rest of the room was filled with bookcases crammed with books. Next to the bed was a tall floor lamp with an old-fashioned fringed shade.

"Looks like reading runs in the family," Kate said as she surveyed the books.

She walked around the room, looking at all of the titles on Annie's shelves. There were rows and rows of books of all kinds, from children's books to science textbooks. They didn't seem to be arranged in any particular order, and there were as many books stacked on the floor as there were on the shelves.

"My parents had a lot of books," Annie said as Kate browsed.

"What do they do?" Kate asked.

"My father was an English professor," Annie answered. "My mother was an artist. Those are her paintings."

Kate looked where Annie was pointing and noticed several large canvases leaning against a wall.

"They're dead," Annie said.

"What?" Kate asked, examining the paintings.

"My parents," Annie said. "They're dead. Meg and I live here with my Aunt Sarah. My father's sister."

"Oh," Kate said. She wasn't sure what she was supposed to say next. Like almost everything she said, Annie mentioned her parents' deaths as if she was simply stating a fact.

Annie turned to one of the bookcases near her bed and picked out a book.

"I guess we should talk about this," she said, tossing the book onto the bed.

Kate sat on the bed and picked up the book. It was a copy of *Spells and Charms for the Modern Witch*. Kate looked up at Annie, who dunked a cookie in her milk, took a bite, and swallowed.

"I got tired of checking it out," she said. "So I bought my own copy. Where should we start?"

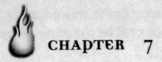

CHAPTER 7

Kate was so stunned that she didn't know where to begin.

"So you *did* try some of the spells," she said accusingly.

Annie nodded. "A few," she said. "But contrary to what you said in the cafeteria, I did *not* use magic to get good grades."

"I'm sorry about that," Kate said. "I just assumed you did because I did."

"You did?" Annie said.

"Don't sound so surprised," Kate said. "It wasn't that hard, really."

"It's just that . . ." Annie began, but let her sentence trail off as she sat on the bed and picked at the patchwork quilt that covered it.

"What?" Kate asked.

Annie sighed. "Well," she tried again. "I said that I *tried* some of the spells."

"And?" Kate said.

"I didn't say they worked," Annie finished,

sounding embarrassed. "At least they didn't work quite the way I wanted them to."

"That's exactly what happened to me!" Kate said. "What happened to yours?"

"You don't want to know." Annie groaned.

"Yes, I do," Kate said. "Now, come on—out with it. It can't be that bad."

Annie made a face. "Oh, yes, it can," she said. "Did you read the part about spells to make it rain?"

"I didn't get that far," Kate admitted.

"I thought it would be a safe way to start," Annie explained. "So I did one, thinking maybe it would snow or something. You know, something harmless."

"And what happened?" Kate asked.

"The pipes in the basement burst," Annie said.

Kate laughed so hard that she thought she might cry. When she was able to speak again, she put her hand on Annie's shoulder.

"If that's the worst thing that happened, then you have nothing to worry about," she said.

"Actually, the mice were worse," Annie said.

"The mice?" Kate asked, wiping her eyes.

"I tried one of the spells for summoning a familiar, too," Annie explained.

"Familiar?" said Kate.

"You really didn't get very far, did you?" Annie said. "Familiars. You know, animals that help witches do their work. Supposedly you can do a spell to summon one. I thought it would be interesting to see what happened."

"And you got mice?" asked Kate.

"Lots of mice," Annie said. "They're still show-ing up in the kitchen, even though I did the spell two months ago. Now, tell me what you did."

Kate explained about the spell for passing her chemistry midterm. "It worked," she said, "but now everyone is mad at me. But that's not nearly as bad as the whole Scott thing."

"The Scott thing?"

Kate sighed. Then she told Annie about making the doll and doing the love spell. "And now all the boys in school are pretty much in love with me," she finished.

"And I thought mice were bad," said Annie. "So, you got a good grade but everyone else failed because of it, and you got not just one boyfriend but fifty or sixty boyfriends. Nice job."

"At least my pipes didn't burst," Kate retorted. "How do we put everything back to normal?"

"You mean make you a marginal student with no love life?" Annie said. "I don't know."

"What do you mean, you don't know!" ex-claimed Kate. "You're the one who read the book a billion times."

"And maybe if you'd read it all the way through even once you wouldn't have gone off making up your own spells," Annie shot back.

The two of them glared at each other for a minute. Then Kate relented. "You're right," she said. "I should have read the whole thing. But after I did the first spell and it seemed to work okay, I thought I could just do what I wanted."

"I haven't learned all that much about witch-craft," Annie said. "But what I have learned is that you have to be careful. This isn't something to just play with. All sorts of things could happen."

"Like mice and ninety-sevens in chemistry," said Kate.

"Exactly," said Annie, picking up the book. "I haven't done any of the spells in here since mine backfired."

"Well, I can't just wait for my problems to go away, or call a plumber or an exterminator to fix them," Kate said. "I need to do something. There's got to be a spell in there that will fix all of this."

Annie began flipping through the book. "I swore I wouldn't try any of this again," she said. "But let's see what's in here."

She flipped through the pages, looking at the spells and rejecting each one. Watching her, Kate got more and more anxious. Annie was her only hope, and if she couldn't find something that would help, Kate didn't know what she would do. But then Annie looked up at her.

"This might just do it," she said.

"What is it?" asked Kate excitedly.

"Well, it's not exactly what you're looking for," Annie said. "It's a ritual for reversing bad luck. But I think it can be reworked a little to fit the occasion."

"Sounds good to me," said Kate. "What do we need to do?"

"We?" said Annie. "What do you mean, we?"

"I thought you were going to help me," Kate said.

"I did help you," Annie said. "I found the spell. But don't expect me to do anything else."

"Come on," said Kate. "You've got to. I can do it myself, but if we both do it, it will be even better."

"No," said Annie, shaking her head emphatically. "Not after last time."

"It might get rid of the last of the mice," Kate said, trying to coax her into cooperating.

Annie groaned. "Fine," she said. "I'll do the spell with you. But that's it."

Kate clapped her hands together triumphantly. "Great. What do we need?"

Annie consulted the book. "The usual," she said, sounding as if she'd done spells a thousand times. "I think I have most of the things we need up here."

She went over to her dresser and pulled open a drawer. There was all kinds of stuff inside. Annie pulled out a box of candles, some matches, a glass jar, and what looked like a metal bowl. She put everything on the floor in the middle of the room.

"I need to get some things from the kitchen and check on Meg," she said. "I'll be right back."

While Annie was gone, Kate took the candles and arranged them in a circle, just as she'd done when performing her own spells. The metal bowl turned out to be a small cauldron with three legs. Kate put it in the center of the circle because that's where it seemed to belong. She put the glass jar next to it. It was filled with some kind of powder, but Kate didn't know what it was. When Annie came back a few minutes later, she looked at Kate's handiwork.

"Perfect," she said. "Now, put this in the circle, too." She handed Kate a box of salt, an empty bowl, and a kitchen knife.

Kate put the items next to the cauldron while Annie turned out the lights and closed the curtains. With the room almost completely dark, it was hard for Kate to see anything at all. But Annie seemed to know her way around, and a moment later she was standing in the circle of candles with Kate.

"Shall we cast the circle?" she said.

"Cast the circle?" Kate said. "You mean light the candles?"

"That's only part of it," Annie said. "You really didn't read any of the book, did you?"

"Not the first half," Kate said. "I kind of skipped right to the spell part."

"That's half your problem right there," Annie said. "Now, watch me."

"Lead on, mouse queen," Kate said.

Annie turned and faced the front of the house. Bending down, she lit one of the candles. Then she raised the knife, holding it with both hands and pointing it in front of her. "East," she said, "creature of air. We ask that you come to our circle."

"What are you doing?" whispered Kate as Annie paused.

"I'm calling the directions," Annie said. "You invite them to the circle."

"Are they here?" asked Kate. She had no idea what Annie was talking about. This was the first she'd ever heard about inviting anyone—or anything—into the circle.

"Just listen," Annie said. "Try to envision the elements as I call them. It's supposed to help."

Kate shut her eyes and thought about air. She imagined winds surrounding her. She pictured herself floating in the sky, held up by invisible hands. She felt the wind on her face and beneath her body. It wasn't nearly as hard as she imagined it would be, and she was almost disappointed when Annie turned to her right and lit another candle.

"South, creature of fire," she said, holding out the knife as she had before. "We ask that you come to our circle."

This time Kate pictured a crackling fire. She held out her hands to it and felt the warmth soaking into her skin. She imagined the shadows of the dancing flames, and she felt as if she was really dancing along with them.

Once more Annie turned and lit a candle. "West," she said, "creature of water. We ask that you join us in our circle."

Kate pictured herself diving into the bluest water she could imagine, and felt it surround her with its cool touch. She imagined a sea without an end to it, stretching all across the world. She visualized the beach that she sometimes rode her bike to, and the way the waves crashed on the sand and then pulled back again. She thought about how the sea was sometimes soothing and sometimes frightening, but always moving.

Annie turned one more time, lighting a fourth candle. "North, creature of the earth," she said. "We ask that you join us in our circle."

Kate shut her eyes and thought about the earth. She pictured mountains stretching up to the sky the way the mountains around Beecher Falls did. She envisioned vast deserts of shifting sands. She recalled the smell of digging in the garden in the summer. She imagined putting her hands into the earth and feeling it between her fingers. Suddenly she felt a sense of being rooted to the ground, as if she were standing in a forest surrounded by trees and growing things.

"Our circle is cast," Annie said, breaking Kate's concentration.

Kate opened her eyes and looked around. Annie was lighting all of the candles that connected the four main ones, and now they were standing in a ring of light.

"That was really weird," Kate said. "I could actually feel the earth, air, fire, and water as you talked about them."

"That's the whole idea," Annie said. "When you cast a circle, you're creating a sacred space for doing magic. You invite the directions, and the elements that represent them, to help you create that space."

"How'd you learn all of this?" Kate asked.

"I told you, I read a lot," Annie said. "It's all in the book. You know, in the part you were supposed to read before you started playing with spells."

"And what's with the knife?" Kate said. "It seems kind of hostile to be pointing a knife at things you're supposed to be inviting to join us."

"The knife is the traditional tool of witches," Annie explained. "You use it to focus your energy. When I was casting the circle, I imagined white light coming from my body and flowing through the knife as I moved it around the circle to create a boundary. But it doesn't have to be a knife. I guess you can use branches or just your hands if you want to."

Annie sat down on the floor, and Kate followed suit. Annie took the little cauldron and put something into it, which she then lit with a match.

"This is incense," she said as she unscrewed the top on the glass jar and reached inside. She took some of the powder inside and sprinkled it into the cauldron. A thick cloud of smoke poured out and the room filled with a strong smell.

"It's sage incense," said Annie as Kate coughed a little. "It's supposed to purify whatever it touches. We're supposed to wave it around our bodies."

Kate fanned the smoke, blowing it around herself. "Well, if anything will get rid of those mice, that will," she muttered.

Annie, ignoring her, took the box of salt and poured some into the empty bowl. She set the bowl between herself and Kate.

"Salt is also a purifying substance," she said. "According to the spell, we're supposed to put our hands in it to get rid of any negative energy that might be hanging around us."

They plunged their hands into the bowl of salt. "Now, repeat after me," Annie said. "Spells and magic gone astray."

Kate repeated the words, and Annie continued. "Turn around and come my way. All gone wrong shall be made right. Return to me, return tonight."

"Now imagine all of the spells you did coming back to you," Annie said, her voice getting deeper and sounding more dreamy as she talked. "Picture them as birds flying back to you and landing on your outstretched hands. Each one is a little piece of magic that you sent out into the world, and now you're calling them home."

Kate imagined herself standing on a green hilltop with her arms out to her sides. One by one, small black birds flew to her and landed on her body. She felt their feet on her skin and heard their wings flutter the air as they settled down.

"Now imagine the birds going to sleep," Annie continued. "One by one they tuck their heads under their wings, until they're all quiet."

"Now what do I do with them?" Kate asked after all of her imaginary birds were sleeping.

"Imagine putting them all into a big birdcage," Annie said. "Sort of like putting them to bed. Take each one and put it in there. When they're all in there, shut the door. It symbolizes all of the magic you sent out into the world being returned to the place it came from."

Kate put all of the little black birds into a big cage in her mind. When they were all inside, she shut the door.

"Is that it?" she asked, looking at Annie.

Annie removed her hands from the bowl of salt and shook them off. "I think so," she said. "I can't really think of anything else."

"There doesn't seem to be much to all of this magic stuff except imagining a lot of things," said Kate. "I thought it would be more about chanting spells and grinding up dried frogs or something."

"It's all about energy," said Annie. "At least that's what I've read. I don't really understand it all, either. But most of the books I've read say that magic is really about sending out energy. You know, like you wanted Scott to ask you out so you imagined him doing it and you sent that energy out into the world to make it happen."

"Next time I'll just ask him out myself," Kate said. "It's a lot easier. So, what will this spell we just did accomplish?"

"It's supposed to put a stop to all the spells you did," Annie said. "But I can't promise anything. Like I said, I don't know much more about this than you do."

"Hey, you knew about inviting all of those directions," Kate said. "At least you had a guest list. I did everything backwards. But I hope all those guys will leave me alone now."

"What if Scott leaves you alone, too?" asked Annie.

"I hadn't thought about that," Kate said, suddenly alarmed. "You don't think he's only with me because of the spell, do you? I'd like to think my charming personality had something to do with it, too."

"I guess we'll find out tomorrow," Annie answered. "But for now we need to open the circle."

"I'll help you blow out the candles," Kate said, leaning over and starting to puff on one.

"No!" Annie shouted, startling Kate. "We have to do it the right way."

She stood up again, holding the knife in the direction she'd ended with when casting the circle. "North, creature of the earth," she intoned. "Thank you for being with us in our circle."

She went around the circle, saying the same thing to each of the directions. When she was done, she told Kate that it was okay to blow out the candles. Then she turned the lights back on and began gathering up all of the items and putting them away.

"So, do you really believe in all of this?" Kate asked as she helped put the candles into the box.

Annie shrugged. "It's hard to say," she answered. "I mean, most of my life has been spent with science. Ever since I was little I've loved it. It makes sense to me. There are rules and formulas and numbers for figuring everything out. You can prove things or disprove them by doing experiments. But this isn't really something you can prove."

"How did you get into it?" Kate asked.

"That's a long story," Annie said. "Right now I have to get this all cleaned up. My aunt will be home soon."

"I'll get going then," Kate said. "It's almost time for dinner anyway."

They put away the last of the things they'd used and picked up their milk glasses and the empty cookie plate. Back down in the kitchen, Annie poured the bowl of salt into the sink and ran water over it.

"It doesn't seem very magical," she said as the salt dissolved and ran down the drain. "But it will have to do."

She got Kate's coat from the closet and gave it to her. As Kate was putting it on, Meg came in from the other room holding her book.

"If you come again, I'll read to you," she said.

"I'd like that," Kate said. "Do you promise to do all the voices for the characters?"

Meg giggled and ducked back into the living room. Kate turned to Annie.

"Thanks," she said.

"No problem," said Annie.

"I meant what I said about coming back," Kate said. "I'd really like to, if it's okay with you."

"Sure," said Annie. "I'd like that. Just promise me one thing."

"What's that?" asked Kate.

"No more spells," Annie said. "I have enough trouble with mice. I don't want a lot of boys running around the kitchen, too."

"I have a feeling that won't be a problem anymore," Kate said. "I think tomorrow is going to be a lot better than today."

Kate left Annie's house and walked home feeling better than she had in days. She was sure that the ritual she and Annie had done would make everything right. She was immensely relieved to have found someone to help her, and Annie seemed to understand her. As she walked, her thoughts reverted to Scott, and she caught herself wondering what his surprise for her was, and then glumly wondered if she'd still even get it. She wasn't sure what to expect from him, if anything.

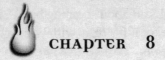

CHAPTER 8

Kate walked into school on Tuesday morning filled with uncertainty. She was sure that she and Annie had managed to fix the spells that had gone wrong and put everything in order again, but she wasn't sure what that meant exactly. So when she saw Scott standing in the hallway as she entered, she smiled nervously and walked over to him.

"There you are," he said. "Are you ready for your surprise?"

Kate breathed a sigh of relief. She'd been so stressed out about what was going on that she hadn't been able to enjoy the thought that he was doing something special for her. But now she couldn't wait to find out what it was.

"Sure," she said. "Show away."

Scott took her by the hand and led her around the corner toward the lockers.

"Ta-da," he said, pointing.

Kate looked in the direction of his gesturing arm. There on the wall was her yearbook picture from the previous year, blown up three times larger than life. It was the focal point of a poster that said: KATE MORGAN FOR VALENTINE'S DAY QUEEN!

"What is that?" Kate asked with growing apprehension.

Scott grinned. "The team nominated you for Valentine's Day queen," he explained. "There are posters all over the school."

Kate had also forgotten about the Valentine's Day dance, and about the voting for queen. Every year at the dance a queen was elected by the student body. All of the different clubs and sports teams were allowed to nominate a candidate, and the winner was announced the night of the dance. The queen then got to choose her Valentine's Day king.

But Kate had a bad feeling about the poster as she stared at it. The football team's candidate was almost always a senior cheerleader. She knew that they'd chosen her because of the spell she'd cast, and that meant that things weren't entirely back to normal after all.

"Isn't it great?" Scott said. "It was a unanimous choice."

"I'm sure it was," Kate said. Then, seeing the confused look on Scott's face, she added, "I'm really happy."

"You're going to win," Scott said confidently. "I mean, how could you lose?"

I wish I knew, Kate thought. *I wish I knew.*

"I've got to get to class," she said to Scott. "I'll see you later, okay?"

"Sure thing," he said. "But don't forget your button."

"My button?" Kate said.

Scott unzipped his backpack and pulled something out. He handed it to Kate. It was a button. Like the poster, it featured her smiling face, and the words "Let Me Be Your Valentine!" were printed around the edges. Kate's heart sank.

"The guys stayed up most of the night making them," Scott said. "We're going to hand them out to everyone. Jeff is already passing them out at the other door."

"Great," Kate said. "Just great."

"I knew you'd love them," Scott said as he pinned one to her shirt.

Kate walked to her locker, waiting until she was around the corner to remove the button and stick it in her pack. It was bad enough that her face was plastered on the walls everywhere she went; she didn't want to be a walking advertisement for herself as well.

"Great posters, Kate," a guy said as he passed her. "Hope you win."

"Thanks," Kate said weakly as she went to her locker.

Several more boys passed her wearing Kate Morgan buttons and wishing her luck. In fact, just about every guy she saw had her face on his shirt.

The girls, though, did not. In fact, most of the girls who passed by her frowned. Kate wanted to apologize to each and every one of them, explaining that it wasn't her fault. But it *was* her fault, and she knew it. It was her fault for working a spell she didn't know how to control. Now she felt like the magic was punishing her somehow by making everything go wrong.

Annie was waiting for her at the lockers. "Congratulations," she said cheerfully.

Kate saw that she was wearing one of the buttons. "Not you, too," she said.

"What?" said Annie, frowning. "This isn't a good thing?"

"Don't you get it?" Kate asked. "It means our spell failed. The boys are paying more attention to me than ever. And if you look around, you'll see that you're the only nonmale in this place sporting one of those things."

"I hadn't thought of that," Annie said as she looked around and saw that Kate was right. "But, hey, maybe it's just some kind of residual effect, you know? Maybe this was all planned before we did our ritual."

Kate paused as she opened her locker. "Maybe," she said, a little bit of hope creeping into her voice. "Maybe this is just the last thing I have to get through and then it will all be over."

Annie peered into Kate's locker. "That's the neatest locker I've ever seen," she said, clearly impressed by the way everything inside was arranged. "And I thought I was compulsive."

"Organization is the key to peace of mind," Kate answered, taking out the books she needed for the morning and reordering the others so they were in the same order as her class schedule. "I should have remembered that when I was doing my spell. Then maybe things wouldn't have gone so wrong. Now, give me that button."

Annie took off the button and handed it to Kate, who threw it into her locker with disgust and shut the door. Then the two of them started toward the chemistry room. As they climbed the stairs to the second floor, they saw a group of girls putting up a poster. It was a picture of Terri Fletcher dressed in a robe and wearing a crown, and the poster said: DON'T BE FOOLED BY PRETENDERS TO THE THRONE—VOTE FOR A REAL QUEEN. Terri was being sponsored by the drama club, and Kate knew exactly who they were talking about when they mentioned pretenders. She walked past the group of girls as quickly as she could, but not before she heard them laughing loudly.

"What did we do wrong?" she asked Annie as they entered the classroom. "I thought things went so well last night."

"It's not like an experiment," Annie said. "You can't measure the results scientifically. I don't know what happened. We'll just have to wait and see."

Kate saw Tara sitting in her usual seat, and for a moment she was torn between sitting with her new friend and sitting with her old one. She felt as if she and Annie now shared something that she didn't share with anyone else. Still, she knew it would look strange if she suddenly began sitting somewhere else. So as Annie went to her seat, Kate put her books down next to Tara.

"Hey," she said as she sat down, testing the waters to see if Tara was still angry at her.

"Hey," said Tara. She didn't sound angry, but she didn't sound exactly friendly, either.

"I see you've got your own poster," Tara said casually.

"Yeah," said Kate. "I didn't know anything about it. Scott surprised me this morning."

"You know, the football team candidate almost always wins," Tara said. "Looks like you're the odds-on favorite now."

"I don't know," Kate said, feeling more and more uncomfortable with the direction the conversation was taking. "It's early. There will be a lot of other candidates people will vote for."

"We'll see," Tara answered. "But the way things are going for you, I wouldn't be surprised."

Kate knew that Tara's last comment was a dig at her for getting a good grade on the midterm, but she ignored it. She was already on really thin ice with her friends, and one false step would send her crashing through. All she could do was wait and hope that maybe the spell she and Annie had done would kick in soon. If it didn't, she wasn't sure what she would do.

Despite her initial hope that things would get better, the day was difficult for her. Everywhere she went she saw her picture smiling down from those awful posters. And it seemed that every boy in the school was wearing her button. Even Mr. Draper and Mr. Niemark, her math teacher, had them on. Only the girls wore Terri's buttons. It was as if the school had divided into two enemy camps, with the boys on Kate's side and the girls on Terri's.

At lunch Kate sat with Scott and his football team buddies, but all they talked about was her campaign for Valentine's Day queen. She pretended to listen, but really she was thinking about Tara, Sherrie, and Jessica, sitting in one part of the cafeteria, and Annie, sitting alone in another. For different reasons, she wanted to be sitting at the other tables, and she felt trapped in the middle. Even the other players' girlfriends had stopped sitting at the football table, but their boyfriends didn't seem to notice.

What's happening here? Kate thought as she ate her lunch without tasting any of it. *Why aren't things going back to normal?* Then she had a horrible thought. Maybe this *was* normal now. Maybe the magic had changed things permanently. Maybe it was the price she had to pay for getting what she wanted.

When school was over, Kate raced home as quickly as she could. Up in her room, she picked up the book of spells and looked at it. "You've caused enough trouble," she said. "Tomorrow you go back to the library, where you belong."

She placed the book in her backpack and went downstairs to help her mother finish making dinner. She was determined to make her life as normal as she possibly could, and that meant staying far away from magic and witchcraft.

For the first time in a long while, both of her parents were home for dinner, and Kate was able to forget about her problems as she busied herself telling them about the upcoming basketball game. She left out the part about being nominated for Valentine's Day queen, and the part about going to the dance with Scott, because she knew they'd be excited for her and she didn't want to have to talk about it. She wanted to feel ordinary, not special. She'd had enough attention for a while. It felt good just to wash dishes, do some homework, and go to bed.

The next morning she had no idea what to expect when she got to school. She half expected to find that someone had erected a statue of her on the school lawn or that the entire school had been renamed after her. Another part of her hoped that, somehow, everything would have gone back to the way it was before she'd ever done a spell.

But the posters of her were still up. Only now there were posters of several other candidates as well. A picture of Terri Fletcher hung a few feet away from one of Kate, and two or three other faces peered out from the walls.

As Kate walked through the halls looking at all the posters, she noticed that while a lot of the boys were still wearing her buttons, some of them were sporting buttons with other faces on them. Fewer of them said hello to her or smiled at her, and she didn't get quite as many hostile looks from other girls as she had been getting. *Maybe it's working*, she thought happily.

Annie was waiting for her again at her locker, and Kate felt a stab of guilt as she found herself hoping that Sherrie, Jessica, and Tara wouldn't see them talking. She still wasn't sure how she was going to handle her friendship with Annie. She really liked her, but she had to admit that Annie was something of a liability when it came to maintaining a reputation.

"Looks like you have some competition," Annie said.

"I know," Kate said. "What do you think it means?"

"Either that our ritual is working or that people *really* don't want you to win," Annie said.

"That makes me feel so much better," Kate said. "Thanks."

"I told you it would take time to know for sure," Annie responded.

"Yeah, well, in the meantime I'm taking this back to the library," Kate said, holding up the spell book. "I want it as far away from me as possible. Want to come with me?"

She and Annie walked to the library. Inside, Kate put the book into the return slot at the desk and let out a sigh of relief as she heard it hit the bottom of the collection box with a dull thud.

"At least that's out of my life," she said as she and Annie left.

As they walked to chemistry, Kate tried not to notice the hostile glances she received from some of the people passing by. As a result, it wasn't until she and Annie were halfway up the stairs that she saw none other than Terri Fletcher coming toward them going the other way. Kate thought about turning around and going back down the stairs before Terri saw her, but it was too late. There were too many people coming up behind her.

As Terri passed Annie halfway down the stairs, she gave a sudden lurch and tumbled forward. Kate watched in horror as Terri's mouth opened in a scream and her hands went out in front of her in an attempt at grabbing the handrail. But it was too late, and a moment later Terri was falling. It all seemed to be happening in slow motion, with Kate frozen and unable to do anything but watch as Terri appeared to fly by her and land on the floor in a heap. When Kate finally came to her senses, her ears were filled with the sound of screaming.

"My ankle!" Terri cried. She was lying at the bottom of the stairs, her books and papers scattered around her like leaves. She was holding her leg, and her face was contorted in pain.

"My ankle!" she wailed again. "I think it's broken."

Several students had rushed over when they heard Terri screaming, and she was surrounded by a growing group. As they bent over her, trying to see what they could do, Terri looked up at Annie and pointed a finger at her.

"She pushed me," Terri said. "I felt her push me."

Like Kate, Annie had stopped when she heard Terri scream. Now she was standing on the stairs looking down at Terri and the others.

"I felt someone push me when I walked by," Terri said. "I know she did it."

At that moment, Sherrie, Jessica, and Tara came around the corner. They saw Terri on the floor, cradling her leg. They saw Kate and Annie standing on the stairs. Kate opened her mouth to say something, but she knew it was too late. She could tell by the looks on their faces that they thought Annie had pushed Terri.

"It was an accident," Kate said helplessly. "She must have slipped."

"No," Terri shouted. "I know she pushed me."

Kate ran up the stairs to where Annie was standing, unmoving. "I think we should get out of here," she whispered, and when Annie didn't move she grabbed her arm. "Come on."

Annie allowed herself to be pulled up the stairs, away from Terri and everyone who was coming to see what had happened.

"I didn't push her," Annie said, leaning against the hallway wall.

"I know that," said Kate. "But no one is going to believe you." She pounded her fist against a nearby locker. "Why is this happening?" she said. "Every time something even remotely good happens, something terrible has to happen right afterward. I don't understand it."

"I think you started something that's gotten out of control," Annie said. "I think the spells you did are magnifying somehow, and the ritual we did to stop them just made things worse."

"But how do we stop it?" Kate asked. "If this keeps up, they'll be tying us to stakes on the front lawn."

"I think we need help," Annie said.

"Help?" said Kate. "Who is there to help us?"

"Well, you came to me because my name was on the list of people who'd checked out the book," Annie said. "I know I wasn't the first one to check it out. Do you remember if there were any other names?"

Kate thought. "I just noticed yours because you'd checked it out so often."

"We have to find out who else has taken that

book out," Annie said. "Let's go to the library."

They couldn't get to the library by going back down the stairs. They could tell there was still a lot of commotion going on, and it sounded as if Terri was still crying. They had to take the long way around. Fortunately, no one who saw them seemed to connect them with what was going on.

"Probably they're all still standing around Terri, listening to her blame you," Kate said.

"At least they're out of our way," Annie responded. "Let's just find the book and get out of here. I hope they've reshelved it already so we don't have to ask for it."

They were in luck. The book had been put back on the shelf. Annie opened it and took out the circulation card.

"There's a signature here," she said, "but I can't read it. It's been crossed out."

"Someone didn't want anyone to know they were reading this," Kate said. "I can't say I blame them."

Annie took a piece of paper out of her notebook and laid it across the circulation card. Then she took her pencil and lightly rubbed it over the paper.

"What are you doing?" Kate asked.

"It's a trick I read about in a mystery novel," Annie said. "You rub the pencil over the paper and the impression of what's underneath shows up."

"How very Nancy Drew," Kate said. She watched

as Annie rubbed, and soon she saw a name emerging through the pencil marks. "Can you read it?" she asked.

Annie held up the paper and looked at it. "It looks like Cocker or Copper or something like that," she said.

Kate thought for a minute. "Could it be Cooper?" she asked.

Annie squinted at the paper. "Maybe," she said. "The writing is really messy. But yeah, it could be Cooper. Cooper Riv-something."

"Rivers," said Kate dully. "Cooper Rivers."

"You don't sound too thrilled," Annie said, putting the card back in the book.

"Cooper Rivers is one of the most antisocial people at Beecher Falls High School," Kate said unenthusiastically. "Her mother teaches in the elementary school. We were in fourth grade together."

"And she pushed you down on the playground or made you eat chalk or what?" Annie asked. "You make her sound like a juvenile delinquent."

"No," said Kate. "She's just kind of strange. You'd probably know her if you saw her. Thin. Short hair that changes color about once a month. Currently pink, I believe. Wears Hello Kitty T-shirts and vinyl pants. Hangs out with the rock-and-roll crowd that smokes behind the building."

"Oh, her," said Annie. "I've seen her around."

"Then you know what I mean when I say she

isn't exactly the most approachable girl in school," Kate said.

"I still think we need to try," Annie said. "I read somewhere that magic grows more powerful when more people are doing it. Something about raising energy and all of that. Maybe Cooper's the thing we need to fix this once and for all. Besides, strange is in the eye of the beholder, remember?"

Kate knew Annie was right. They had to try something. They hadn't been able to reverse her spells by working together. Maybe they did need someone else. But Cooper Rivers? If Kate and Annie were unlikely candidates for trying out witchcraft, Cooper was even more of a long shot. Still, they were running out of options. And Annie was right about not making assumptions. Maybe Cooper wasn't all that bad.

"All right," Kate said. "But you do all the talking."

"Fine," said Annie. "So, where do we find this Cooper Rivers?"

"My guess is one of the music rooms," Kate said. "She's really into playing the guitar."

The school's music rooms were in the basement. Kate and Annie walked down the row of doors trying to peer through the small panes of glass that served as windows to see who was inside. Finally, near the end of the row, Kate stopped.

"That's her," she said.

Annie looked in and saw a girl sitting on a stool, a guitar in her hands. A pair of headphones sat on her head, pushing down her hair, which was indeed dyed bright pink. She was mouthing some words, and her eyes were closed.

"Here goes nothing," Annie said, and pushed open the door.

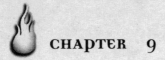

CHAPTER 9

"You'd better have a really good reason for doing that," Cooper Rivers said as Annie and Kate barged into the practice room. At the sound of the door opening, she'd stopped singing and looked up to see what was going on. "I just about had the last lyric I need to finish my song."

"Sorry to interrupt," Annie said.

"Yeah, sorry," added Kate. "We didn't mean to ruin your concentration."

"Great. Now that we've established that, can I get back to what I was doing?" Cooper started to put her headphones back on, but Annie began talking.

"Wait," she said. "We need to talk to you."

Cooper rolled her eyes. "No, I don't want to buy candy bars to support the chorus," she said. "No, I don't want to sign a petition trying to get the cafeteria to go vegetarian. No, I don't want to get involved in student government. 'Bye now."

Annie looked at Kate. "What do you know about witchcraft?" Annie said to Cooper.

Cooper stared at them for a moment without saying anything. Kate held her breath, waiting to hear the response. Cooper looked at Annie, then at Kate.

"Nothing," she said sharply. "Now, get out of here and let me get back to my song."

"I think you do," Annie said, staying put. Kate was surprised at how forceful Annie was being. She would have been happy to leave Cooper alone. But Annie was pushing.

"Look," said Cooper. "I don't know who you are. I don't *care* who you are. And I don't know anything about what you're talking about."

"You mean about *witchcraft*?" Annie said, emphasizing the last word.

"Right," said Cooper, meeting her gaze. "About that."

"Well, we do," Annie said. "We've been doing some spells."

Kate was horrified that Annie had given out so much information to Cooper, who clearly didn't want anything to do with them. Cooper didn't respond to Annie. She just sat there, her green eyes revealing nothing and her guitar resting against her hip.

"We've been doing some spells," Annie said again. "And they haven't been coming out quite right."

"Sorry to hear it," Cooper said sarcastically. "Maybe you should ask Santa and the Easter Bunny to help you out."

Kate could tell that the conversation was going nowhere. "Come on, Annie," she said. "We made a mistake. Let's go."

"We didn't make a mistake," Annie said. "She's just scared."

"What are you talking about?" Cooper said angrily.

"You're scared," Annie said. "I don't know why, but I know you are."

"You're out of your mind," Cooper said. "I don't even have the first clue what you're talking about. There's no such thing as witchcraft."

"That's where you're wrong," Annie said. "It's real. And I think you know that. But if you don't want to help us, that's up to you."

Kate waited for Cooper to respond. A long minute went by during which no one spoke. Finally, Cooper said, "Sorry. Like I said, I can't help you. Try someone else."

"We don't need someone else," Annie replied. "We need you. If you want to help us, come to this address Friday night at nine. We'll be there." She ripped out a piece of notebook paper, wrote her address on it, and held it out to Cooper. Cooper didn't take it.

"You've got the wrong girl," she said. "Keep it."

Annie folded the paper in half and tossed it into the open guitar case at Cooper's feet. "Just in case you know who the right person is," she said.

Kate and Annie left the practice room, closing

the door behind them. Annie was angry, and as they walked down the hallway she kept stopping and turning, as if she wanted to go back.

"I know she's the one," she said, balling her hands into fists. "I just know it."

"What do you mean, she's the one?" Kate asked, not understanding. "The one what?"

"The one we need," Annie said. "There's a reason her name is in that book, and there's a reason we need her help. Just like there was a reason for you to come ask me for help."

"A lot of good that did," Kate said, leaning against the wall.

"Yeah, well, it was nice meeting you, too," Annie said.

"Calm down," Kate said, surprised at the vehemence of Annie's response. "You know what I meant. Why are you so mad about this?"

"Because that girl knows something," Annie said, still fuming. "She knows something, and she's holding out on us. We've got to get her to come to my house Friday night."

"Right now we need to get to class," Kate said. "I just hope the whole thing with Terri has settled down a little."

The thing with Terri had not settled down. Within half an hour of her accident, the story had spread all over school, and the most popular version of the story had Annie shoving Terri and then running away. It hadn't helped any that Kate and Annie had both skipped chemistry. That just made Annie look even more guilty, and for the rest of the day Kate felt like she was harboring a known criminal.

"I can't believe you're standing up for that freak," Sherrie said at lunch. "You were there. You saw what happened. There's no way Terri just fell. Someone pushed her."

"I'm telling you, Annie wouldn't do that," Kate said, wishing she'd decided to sit with Scott like he'd asked.

Kate didn't know what else to say. She knew that Annie had had nothing to do with Terri's accident. But if she tried to defend her, Sherrie and the others would think that Kate had done it. Everything was falling apart, and there didn't seem to be any way to fix it.

"Face it, Kate," Jessica said. "You have a stalker."

"What?" asked Kate.

"A stalker," Jessica repeated. "This Annie wants to be just like you, so she's trying to impress you by taking out your competition. I saw a movie like this on Lifetime once. Valerie Bertinelli played this single mom who was really nice to a baby-sitter she hired to watch her kids. The next thing she knew, all of her neighbors were turning up dead."

Kate knew that nothing she could say would make her friends think anything but what they already believed. She took a bite of her sandwich and chewed it furiously. She knew that Annie was eating lunch by herself, but she didn't dare even turn around to look for her. Getting back into her friends' good graces had been hard enough; she couldn't risk alienating them again.

As she ate, her thoughts turned toward Cooper Rivers. Annie was so sure that Cooper was the missing piece of the puzzle. But how could she know that? She hadn't even known who Cooper was until Kate had told her. Yet she had seemed almost frantic to get Cooper to talk to them earlier. Did Cooper really know something, or was Annie just grasping at straws? Kate didn't have a clue. She'd been through so many ups and downs in the past week that she didn't know what to think anymore.

"Earth to Kate," she heard someone say, and immediately all thoughts of Cooper went out of her head.

"What?" she said.

Sherrie, Jessica, and Tara were staring at her.

"I asked what you and lover boy are going to the dance as," Sherrie said.

"Oh," said Kate. "I don't really know yet. We haven't had a lot of time to discuss it." Of course, she had already talked about it with Scott, but she didn't want anyone to know what her idea was yet. She wanted it to be a surprise.

"Well, you'd better decide pretty soon," Sherrie said. "The dance is next Saturday night. We're going shopping for costumes this weekend. You're coming, right?"

"Sure," Kate said, trying to sound cheerful. "Definitely."

"Good," said Sherrie. "It will be the old gang together again."

"We were starting to worry about you a little," Jessica said to Kate. "You know, what with all of your new interests. We thought maybe you didn't want to hang with us anymore."

"What new interests?" Kate said.

"You know, Scott and studying for chemistry tests," Tara said. "We haven't seen much of you lately."

"I'm sorry," Kate said. "I've just been really busy. But I promise this weekend we'll all hang out."

"We can start Friday night," Jessica said. "We're having a sleepover at my house."

"Oh, I can't do Friday night," Kate said. "I have other plans. Sorry."

Her three friends looked at her. "Other plans?" Sherrie said. "They wouldn't happen to involve a big stupid football player, would they?"

"No," Kate said, anxious to keep the peace. "They wouldn't. I have to do something with my parents. But I'm definitely on for Saturday shopping."

"You're the only person I know who spends Friday night with her parents," Tara said. "I'm not sure if I think that's cool or insane."

Again, Kate felt terrible about lying to her

friends. But there was no way she could tell them that she was staying over at Annie's house. They'd think she was a traitor for sure, and until she and Annie were able to fix whatever had gone wrong with the spells, she wasn't taking any more chances. Besides, she really did miss her friends. The past few days had been hard on her.

Maintaining an appearance of innocence meant not speaking to Annie for the rest of the day. Several times Kate passed her in the hallway going to and from classes, but Annie just walked by as if she'd never seen Kate before. Kate did the same, and every time she did it made her feel worse. She had to listen to people talking about Annie everywhere she went, and she couldn't say a word in Annie's defense.

The only good thing to come out of the accident involving Terri was that, for a change, people weren't talking about Kate. And although she hated having to watch her friend suffer, Kate was also a little bit relieved at not being the one everyone was staring at and spreading rumors about. People seemed to think that Annie was just trying to impress Kate by harming Terri. Several students even came up to tell her how sorry they were.

"It must be awful," said a girl Kate recognized as one of the girls who had confronted her a few days before about flirting with the boys.

"You have no idea," said Kate. As she watched the girl walk away, she thought, *It's like they're all bewitched. One day they're accusing me of trying to steal their boyfriends, and the next they've forgotten all about it and are ready to blame Annie for Terri's accident.*

Everything seemed to be spinning out of control. It was almost as if the magic had taken on a life of its own once she'd set it loose. She knew that Annie hadn't pushed Terri, but *something* had happened on that stairway. Terri hadn't just fallen. Something had made her fall. And if it hadn't been Annie, then what had it been? Was it possible that the magic was doing everything? And how could they stop it before things really started getting dangerous? Were she and Annie carrying around some kind of negative energy that could cause people to have accidents? If magic really was energy, maybe it could act like static electricity, zapping people when they got too close. The idea that she might be able to cause even more damage made Kate feel sick to her stomach. For the first time since she'd opened the spell book, she felt afraid. She'd thought that magic was harmless, but now she wasn't sure.

Kate had basketball practice that afternoon, and all anyone could talk about was Terri Fletcher and Annie Crandall. Kate was so tired of hearing the story of Terri's fall repeated over and over that when she was done practicing she dressed and left, telling Tara and Jessica that she had to help her mother get ready for a catering event.

As soon as she was home she went to her room,

picked up the phone, and dialed Annie's number.

"How are you doing?" she asked when Annie answered.

"Okay," Annie said. "But I got called down to Principal Browning's office this afternoon. She wanted to know what happened."

"What did you tell her?" Kate asked.

"The truth," said Annie. "I told her that I was walking up the stairs, Terri was walking down the stairs, and that I didn't know how she managed to fall."

"Did she believe you?" Kate said.

"I don't think so," Annie replied. "But there was nothing she could do about it. She kept telling me how much pain Terri was in, as if that would make me confess."

"I'm really sorry, Annie," Kate said. "I know you wouldn't be involved in any of this if I hadn't dragged you into it."

"It's okay," Annie said. "It really is. After all, you and I became friends because of it."

"I'm afraid I don't feel much like a friend," Kate answered. "Ignoring you in the halls. Pretending I don't really know you."

"Just think of it as a game," Annie said. "Eventually it will all be over, and then things can be normal."

"Will it ever be over?" Kate said. "We've tried everything we can think of, and nothing seems to be working."

"We have to keep trying," Annie said.

"You mean another ritual?" said Kate. "I'm not sure that's a good idea."

"Not if we do it ourselves," Annie said. "But maybe if we get Cooper to do it with us . . ."

"Forget it," Kate said. "She's not going to help. You heard her this morning. She said she doesn't know anything about witchcraft. I bet she checked out the book, decided it was a lot of nonsense, and returned it without trying anything in it. If I were her, I'd pretend not to know anything, too."

"I still think she knows more than she's letting on," Annie said stubbornly.

"Well, I have homework to do," Kate said, trying to change the subject. "I should go."

"Right," said Annie. "Well, I guess we won't be able to talk much for the next few days, at least at school. We're still on for Friday night, right?"

"I wouldn't miss it," Kate said.

After hanging up, Kate spent the rest of the night working on her math homework and trying to not think about magic and spells. Trying to make the figures on her paper do what she wanted them to do was a good way to distract herself, and when she finally went to bed she had succeeded in feeling almost normal again.

CHAPTER 10

The next two days crawled by. The rumors about Annie continued to spread, and Kate had to force herself not to say anything to her friends that would upset the delicate truce they seemed to have formed. Letting them think that Annie was some kind of out-of-control Kate wannabe was her only option, but it was one that tore her up inside. She really liked Annie. They were different in many ways, and probably would never have met if it hadn't been for the spell book, but they shared something important.

Kate wanted to help her friend, but all she could do was stand by and watch Annie try to get through the days with people talking about her. Already shy, Annie drew even more into herself. She walked silently from class to class, looking at the floor and trying to avoid the stares and comments from the other students.

On Thursday, one of the senior boys pretended to fall when Annie walked by him in the hallway, and everyone around burst into laughter. Kate, who was walking with Jessica, Tara, and Sherrie, watched as Annie turned to say something to the boy, thought better of it, and then fled down the hallway as the laughter followed behind her.

"Don't you have anything better to do?" someone said, interrupting the laughter.

Kate looked around for the speaker and saw Cooper Rivers staring down the boy who had pretended to fall. Everyone was looking at her.

"What's your problem?" one of the girls said sarcastically. "You her bodyguard or something?"

"I think the real question is what *your* problem is," Cooper retorted. "All of you. I swear, if any of you actually had an independent thought your heads would explode."

She stormed off, leaving everyone staring after her. As she passed Kate and her friends she shot Kate a withering look, as if to say, "I know what you're doing, and you make me sick."

"Wow," said Sherrie. "What a couple of freaks those two are."

Kate kept quiet. She knew that everyone was probably thinking what Sherrie was thinking about Annie and Cooper. But Annie was her friend, and Annie thought that Cooper could help them. *I guess that makes me a freak too*, Kate thought as she resumed walking to her class.

By the time Friday afternoon came, Kate was completely miserable. All her friends could talk about was their upcoming shopping trip for costumes, but all she could think about was how things were falling apart. The "Crandall Scandal," as everyone had taken to calling it, was in high gear. Annie was the school pariah, and Kate knew that it was all her fault. To make things even worse, she had absolutely no idea what she could do to fix things. The magic didn't seem to be working. Maybe, she thought, she had only one spell in her and she had used it up getting Scott to notice her.

And the whole thing with Scott was just making everything harder. While the rest of her life was a disaster, things with him were going really well. When he was walking her to class or talking to her at lunch, she felt incredibly special and lucky. Part of her even felt proud that she had managed to get him to pay attention to her. But every time she started feeling happy, a moment later her joy was dampened by the thought of how Annie must be feeling.

Part of her didn't want to go to Annie's house that night. But she knew she owed it to her friend, so she threw some things into a bag and headed over.

When she knocked on the door, it was opened by a woman with long dark hair and a kind face.

"You must be Kate," she said. "Come on in. Annie's in the kitchen."

"Thanks," Kate said as she stepped inside. "You must be Annie's Aunt Sarah."

"Yes," the woman answered as they walked to the kitchen. "It's good to meet you. Annie's told me a lot about you. So has Meg. She's been dying to read to you ever since you were last here."

When she entered the kitchen, Kate smelled something wonderful. Annie was at the stove, stirring something in a big pot that was the source of the enticing aroma.

"Hi," she said. "I hope you like vegetable curry."

"If it tastes as good as it smells, I will," Kate said. "How are you doing?"

Annie shrugged. "As good as can be expected, I guess. I mean, it wasn't like I was Miss Popularity before or anything."

"I really wish I knew what to do," said Kate.

Annie smiled. "Don't worry," she said. "We'll figure something out. But right now it's time for dinner."

Annie's aunt came back with Meg in tow and they all sat down. As Annie dished out the curry and the salad bowl went around the table, Meg chattered happily about the book she'd been reading. Kate was swept up in Meg's enthusiasm, and she quickly forgot about her troubles. The curry was delicious, and she complimented Annie on it as she helped herself to seconds.

"I like to cook," Annie said. "It's kind of like chemistry. You put things together and see how they react."

"Annie inherited her cooking abilities from her

mother," Sarah said. "Chloe could make the most amazing dishes out of whatever was left in the refrigerator."

At the mention of her mother, Annie seemed to become quieter. For the rest of dinner she spoke very little, and the conversation was taken up mostly by Meg's description of something she'd done in school that day. When everyone was finished, Aunt Sarah took Meg upstairs with her and Kate helped Annie clean up.

"Your aunt is really nice," Kate said. All through dinner she'd been wondering what had happened to Annie's parents, and she was hoping Annie would volunteer the information.

"Yeah," said Annie. "I don't know what Meg and I would have done without her. She's really the only family we have left."

"It must be hard not having your mom around, though," Kate said, not knowing how else to bring the subject up.

"I guess," said Annie. "It's been so long now that I really don't remember."

Kate wanted to ask Annie more about her mother and about how her parents had died, but Annie didn't seem to want to talk about it.

They finished the dishes, then went up to Annie's room and shut the door. Outside the windows the moon was shining brightly in the clear winter sky, and it filled the room with cold light.

"It's at the first quarter," Annie said, standing at

the window and looking out. "Next week it will be full."

Kate sat on a big chair by the door. "You never did tell me why you checked out that book in the first place," she said. "Or why you bought your own copy."

Annie turned away from the window and came over to the bed. She sat down on the edge and put her hands in her lap. For a minute she didn't say anything. Then she sighed.

"When Meg and I came to live here with Aunt Sarah, I was really sad," she said. "So I disappeared into books. I spent almost all of my time up here reading so that I wouldn't have to talk to anyone."

"That sounds lonely," Kate said, feeling sorry for Annie.

"Not really," said Annie. "I liked reading. Opening a book was like opening a doorway into another world. I could be anyone I wanted to be and go anywhere I wanted to go. I particularly liked fairy tales, maybe because so many of the girls in them have lost their parents somehow. Whatever it was, I read a lot of them, and I was always fascinated by the witches. They seemed so interesting, even when they were supposed to be evil. I guess it sounds stupid, but I wanted to find out if they really existed. So I started reading about witchcraft."

"And you found the spell book?" said Kate.

"Not for a while," Annie said. "I sort of gave up on witches when I got a little older. By then I'd discovered science, and that made a lot more sense than fairies and magic and enchanted castles. But part of me was still curious, and one day when I was looking for books in the library I found the spell book."

"Which one did you try first?" asked Kate.

Annie laughed. "I didn't try any of them for a long time," she said. "In fact, that's really why I checked it out so many times. It took me that long to get up the nerve to actually try one. Finally I got embarrassed about renewing it so many times, so I bought my own copy."

"Where did you find one?" said Kate.

"At this bookstore downtown," Annie said. "I must have walked around the block twenty times before I went inside. I don't know why, but I was really nervous. But I did go in, and I bought the book. Then I did my first spell. It was one about driving away negativity, and it seemed to work. That's when I tried the others, and you know what happened with them."

"Right," said Kate. "The mice."

"And that's pretty much the whole story," said Annie. "I didn't do any more spells until you showed up."

They were silent for a moment. Then Kate asked, "Do you think you're a witch?"

Annie looked at her and started to speak, but she was interrupted by a knock on the bedroom door.

"It's probably Aunt Sarah with hot chocolate," said Annie. "She's big on making it before bedtime."

Annie went to the door and opened it. Her aunt was indeed standing there, and she was carrying a tray with three steaming mugs on it. "I thought you and your friends might like some cocoa," she said.

"Friends?" said Annie. "It's just me and Kate."

"There's one more," her aunt said, coming into the room. Annie saw that there was someone standing behind her in the shadows. The figure stepped forward, and Cooper Rivers was framed in the doorway. She was carrying a backpack, shaped like a fuzzy pink rabbit, that dangled from her hand.

"Sorry I'm a little late," she said. "Has the party already started?"

Annie looked back at Kate, who couldn't believe her eyes.

"No, you're just in time," Annie said. "Come on in."

Cooper stood just inside the door while Annie's aunt put the mugs of cocoa on Annie's dresser and turned to go. "You girls have fun," she said. "I'll see you in the morning."

"What are you doing here?" Kate demanded as soon as the door was shut.

Cooper looked at the mugs of cocoa steaming on the dresser. She seemed to be thinking about what to say next. "Maybe I was afraid one of you would push me down the stairs if I didn't come," she said.

"That's not funny," said Annie.

"Sorry," said Cooper. "Humor's a defense mechanism. You know, to cover up all of my antisocial tendencies and fear of rejection. At least that's what the therapist I saw once said. But I think he was projecting."

Cooper looked from Annie to Kate, as if expecting a response. When she didn't get one she took a deep breath. "Okay," she said. "I wasn't going to come, but I changed my mind."

"Why would you change your mind?" Kate asked.

"Maybe I'm curious," Cooper said after a long pause.

"Curious about what?" Annie asked.

Cooper brushed her hair out of her eyes. "It's not every day someone asks you if you know anything about casting spells," she said.

Kate turned around and looked at Cooper. "And do you?" she said.

"Maybe I do," Cooper said. "But I still don't see what business it is of yours."

"You're impossible," Kate said. "Why are you here if you don't want to talk about it?"

"This would be a little easier if the two of you would stop fighting," Annie said. "Cooper, please sit down and let's talk about this."

Cooper and Kate eyed one another suspiciously, as Cooper settled on one of the many cushions strewn around the room. Kate remained in the chair by the door and Annie was on the bed.

"All right," she said. "Now that we're all at least in the same room, we can start to figure things out. Cooper, Kate and I came to you because we saw your name in a book we had both checked out of the library. Now, we need to know—did you really check it out?"

Cooper hesitated. "Yes," she said. "I checked it out."

"Finally, she admits it," Kate said. "Hallelujah."

"I didn't say I tried anything in it," said Cooper defensively.

"Well, we did try some of the things in it," said Annie. "And nothing worked the way we thought it would. In fact, we've gotten ourselves into some trouble."

"So you really did push that drama queen down the stairs," Cooper said, grinning wickedly. "Who would have thought?"

"No!" Annie said emphatically. "That was an accident. But it is part of the problem. Basically, we did some spells that backfired."

"Mostly mine backfired," Kate admitted. "Annie got dragged into it because I asked her for help."

"So what do you need me for?" Cooper asked.

"We were hoping maybe you had done some of the spells, too," Annie said. "And we were hoping that yours came out a little better than ours did."

"How would that help you?" said Cooper.

"Annie has this idea that if we can work as a

group—sort of join forces—we can stop what seems to be happening," said Kate. She hated admitting to Cooper that she'd screwed up, but she had no choice.

"You two have no idea what you're playing with, do you?" said Cooper.

"And you do?" Kate shot back. She hated being talked down to, and Cooper was doing exactly that.

"Yeah," said Cooper. "Maybe I do. And what I know is that you shouldn't go around playing with things you don't understand, because you can get into a lot of trouble."

"Oh, now suddenly you're the great expert on magic?" said Kate. "A few minutes ago you didn't know anything about it."

"I know enough," said Cooper.

"Then will you help us?" Annie asked. "Please, we don't know who else to go to. We're not asking you to be our friend. We just need to know if there's anything we can do to stop all of this and make things normal again."

Cooper looked down at the floor, sitting in silence while Kate and Annie exchanged glances and wondered what she was thinking about. Then Cooper looked up at them and sighed. "Okay," she said. "I'll do it. I hate to think of the danger you two are likely to unleash if left unattended."

"Thanks," said Annie, smiling. "Now, tell us what you know."

"I think I need some hot chocolate first," said

Cooper, standing up and taking a mug from the dresser. Then she sat back down on the cushion and took a sip while Annie got the other two mugs and handed one to Kate.

"Like I said, I checked out that book," Cooper said. "Let's just say I had some interest in finding out what was in it. But it's pretty much useless."

"What do you mean?" asked Kate. Her initial dislike of Cooper hadn't faded entirely, but she was intrigued by what the other girl had to say.

"Well, some of it is okay," Cooper continued. "But the author pieced it together from a lot of other books. It's hard to separate the good stuff from the bad stuff. It's the kind of book bought by people who talk to crystals and listen to too much Stevie Nicks music."

"And how do you know so much about witchcraft?" asked Annie.

"Let's just say it runs in the family," Cooper said cryptically. "Why don't you tell me what exactly you did."

Annie and Kate took turns telling Cooper which spells they'd done and what had happened. When they were done, she looked at them and shook her head. "Kind of like the sorcerer's apprentice," she said.

"The what?" asked Kate.

"The sorcerer's apprentice," Cooper said. "You know, that story where the sorcerer goes away for the day and his apprentice decides to use his magic wand to get all his chores done. Only everything goes wrong, and the place ends up trashed. It's what happens when people play with magic and don't know how to use it properly."

"You keep talking as if you know so much about all of this," Kate said. "But you never tell us why or how."

"Like I said before," Cooper said. "It's in my genes. The real question is what we're going to do about the mess you two have made."

"Do you have any ideas?" asked Annie.

"I'm not really sure," Cooper admitted. "But I think I know a good place to start looking. Do you know a store called Crones' Circle?"

"That's where I bought my copy of the book," Annie said. "Why?"

"I think we need to pay them a little visit tomorrow," Cooper said.

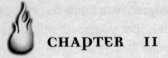

CHAPTER II

The next morning, after a quick breakfast, they were standing at the bus stop waiting for the bus to take them to the downtown shopping area.

"What exactly are we looking for?" Kate asked as the bus stopped and they got on.

"Information," said Cooper, settling into a seat. "We need to find a way to stop or reverse what you two started."

"Why can't we just make something up?" Kate asked.

"Because that's what got you into trouble in the first place," Cooper responded. "You can't just do whatever you want to. You need to follow certain rules."

"But I did follow the rules," Annie said. "And things still came out wrong."

"Maybe you just need a little more practice," Cooper suggested. "You can't be expected to hit a home run your first time at bat."

"You keep talking as if this is something we're

going to keep doing," Kate said. "Don't you get it? We just want this over with. Right, Annie?"

Cooper looked at Annie. "Is that right?" she asked.

"I guess so," Annie answered, but she didn't sound sure.

They sat in silence for a while as the bus moved through the winter morning, stopping every so often to let people on or off as they left the college area and entered downtown Beecher Falls with its streets filled with shops of all kinds. As they passed Kate's father's sporting goods store she saw him through the big front window, animatedly waving his hands around as he showed a customer a backpack.

They got off four stops later, close to the town's waterfront. Kate loved this part of town. The sea air smelled wonderful, and the sound of gulls flying around looking for scraps of food filled the air. She put her hands in her coat pockets and enjoyed the feel of the sun on her face as they walked along.

Cooper led the way down the street and into a narrow lane that Kate had never really noticed before. Halfway down they came to Crones' Circle. It was a small store sandwiched between a coffee shop on one side and a bakery on the other. The sign outside depicted three old women wearing black robes and holding hands as they stood around a cauldron. A full moon hung over their heads. The door to the shop was painted to look like it was covered with ivy.

Cooper pushed the door open and a little bell rang as the three girls walked inside. The first thing Kate noticed was that the air was rich with the smell of incense. The second thing she noticed was a fat gray cat sleeping on the counter by the cash register. The cat opened one eye and looked at them, then seemed to go back to sleep.

The store reminded Kate of what she had always imagined a witch's cottage would look like. The floor was bare wood, and the walls were painted a smoky purple color. Near the back of the store there was a small table covered with a white cloth on which sat some kind of statue of a woman and several lit candles. The entire place was filled with shelves of books. But there were other things as well. Behind the counter there were glass jars filled with herbs of all kinds. Another shelf held candles in tall glass holders. There were bundles of incense sticks, baskets of different colored silk cords, and even a rack of CDs.

But the books were what interested Kate the most. There were so many of them. As she wandered through the store she saw books about dream interpretation, Tarot cards, and herbal healing. Every book seemed more interesting than the last one, and she wanted to open them all and see what they had to say. Then she turned a corner and found herself in a section of books all about witchcraft.

There were books of spells, like the book she'd checked out of the library. There were books about rituals and ceremonies. Kate had never seen so many books about witches before, and she just stood there, staring at them all.

"I don't even know where to start," she said to Annie and Cooper, who had come to stand next to her and were also looking at the books.

"Maybe I can help," said a voice behind them. Kate turned to see a woman standing there. She was tall and thin, and she was wearing a gauzy blue skirt and a loose black shirt printed with orange and yellow fish designs. Her dark hair hung to her waist, and her arms were covered in silver bracelets of all kinds. Her dark eyes sparkled, and Kate liked her almost immediately.

"Do you work here?" Kate asked.

"I'm one of the owners," the woman said. "My name is Sophia. What kind of witchcraft are you interested in?"

"I don't know, really," said Kate. She looked at Annie and Cooper for help.

"We're interested in Wicca," Cooper said confidently.

The woman smiled. "Well, there are all kinds of Wicca," she said. "People tend to use the terms 'witchcraft' and 'Wicca' to mean the same thing, but actually there are many different types."

Cooper looked annoyed, as if she'd been shown up. "What do you suggest then?" she asked.

Sophia turned to the shelves. "Well, there are some really good basic books about the different kinds of witchcraft," she said. "I usually suggest that people read several of them and decide what interests them the most before they do any in-depth exploration. What have you read so far?"

"Not much," admitted Annie when neither Kate nor Cooper spoke up. "We're kind of new to all of this, and we're just looking for some basic information."

"Well, then, I can suggest a few things," Sophia said. "This one here is one of the most familiar books about the Goddess religion," she said as she held up a book with a blue-spiral cover.

"Religion?" said Kate. "Witchcraft is a religion?"

Sophia nodded. "Yes, absolutely," she said. She pulled a book from the shelf and handed it to Kate. "Here's one that has some solid background information. It's a great place to begin. I might also recommend this one over here as well. They both give good, but different, perspectives on how some people practice."

"What about spells?" Cooper said, speaking up. "What spell books do you recommend?"

"I don't recommend any spell books to people who are just starting out," Sophia said kindly. "Magic isn't something you should just leap into. You need to understand the basics first."

Kate hoped she didn't look as embarrassed as she felt. She'd had no idea that there was so much to know about witchcraft. She hadn't even known there were different kinds, or that it was a religion. It had all just seemed like something to do. She felt even more in over her head than she had before she walked in.

"What if you've already sort of tried some spells?" Annie said hesitantly.

Sophia looked thoughtfully at them. "I guess that would depend on what kind of spells they were and how well they turned out."

"Suppose they didn't turn out all that well," Annie said.

"Or too well," Kate added. "Say, for example, you wanted to sort of take back a spell that was doing more than you wanted it to."

"That's a hard one," Sophia said. "Magic is really just a kind of energy. When you do a spell, you're sending that energy out into the world."

"Like when you cast a circle," Annie said.

Sophia nodded. "Right," she said. "That's one kind of energy. Spells involve another kind of energy that we call intention. When you cast a spell, you focus your intention on a specific goal."

"Like getting someone to fall in love with you," Kate suggested, hoping she wasn't giving away too much.

"You could do that," Sophia said. "But I wouldn't recommend it. There are spells for helping you find love, but actually getting someone to fall in love with you is another thing. That kind of magic is manipulative. You're trying to get someone to do something he or she might not do otherwise. That's asking for trouble."

"What kind of trouble?" asked Kate, not at all sure she really wanted to hear the answer.

"Witches believe in what we call the Law of Three," Sophia explained. "We believe that whatever kind of energy you send out into the universe will come back to you three times as strong. For example, if you do a spell to help heal someone, we believe that eventually you will receive healing energy of some sort yourself, and that it will be three times as strong as the energy you sent out."

"And if you do a love spell?" said Kate.

Sophia smiled. "You never know," she said. "Sometimes you find that too many people fall in love with you. Other times you get what you want, but you pay a price for it. A very dear price."

Kate could definitely relate to that. She'd gotten way more than she'd bargained for from her two attempts at magic. "So if you send out an intention to get someone to fall in love with you, you can't take it back?" she asked.

"Not really," said Sophia. "As I said earlier, you've sent that energy out into the world. Now it's out there. Getting it back would be like trying to push electricity back into an outlet. But you *could* try to neutralize the energy from a spell you've cast."

"How do you do that?" asked Annie.

"It takes a lot of concentration," Sophia said. "The best way is to do a ritual in which you thank the universe for accepting the magic that you've sent out and ask that it return the energy to the place it came from. But you also have to make sure that you do everything you can yourself to fix whatever has gone wrong. Magic is a two-part process. Part of it involves asking the universe for help and focusing your energies to make things happen. The other part involves doing whatever nonmagical things you can do to make what you want to happen actually happen. Magic isn't a wishing well you can just keep dipping into whenever you want something. It's something you do in addition to making things happen for yourself."

"This ritual," Annie said. "The one to return energy to the place it came from. Does it work better with more than one person?"

"It can," Sophia answered. "A group of people working magic together can raise very powerful amounts of energy. That's the principle behind a coven."

"I read about covens," Kate said, thinking about her history paper research. "They're groups of thirteen witches, right?"

"That's the number most people think of," Sophia said. "But a coven doesn't have to have a set number of members. Some have thirteen, but others have as few as two or as many as twenty or more. My own coven has nine members at the moment, but we started with three and have had as many as eleven."

"You're in a coven?" said Cooper, who had remained silent while everyone else talked.

"Yes," Sophia said. "In fact, several members of the coven own this store together."

"Then you're a witch," said Kate.

"For twenty years," said Sophia. "In fact, I started practicing Wicca when I was about your age—although, back then there weren't as many books about the Craft and it was harder to get solid information."

Sophia was using so many different names: Wicca, witchcraft, the Craft. Kate wanted to ask her whether they were all the same thing or different things. But just then the bell over the door to the shop rang, and Sophia excused herself to go help the new customer, leaving the girls to look at the books by themselves.

"I like her," Kate said. "She's the first real witch I've ever met."

"She's okay," Cooper allowed.

Annie winked at Kate. "Cooper's just mad because Sophia knows more than she does about Wicca."

Cooper snorted, and the other girls laughed. "I guess we should get these books," Annie said, looking at the books Sophia had suggested. "Then we can go back to my place and look through them."

Kate glanced at her watch. It was already noon.

"I have to get going," she said. "I promised my friends I'd meet up with them, and I'm late."

Cooper and Annie looked confused.

"I mean Sherrie and my other friends," Kate said, feeling terrible about her slipup. "I told them I'd go costume shopping with them. You know, for the Valentine's Day dance."

"I can't believe you'd go to something that lame," Cooper said. "It's just a bunch of sad and lonely losers looking to hook up with other sad and lonely losers of the opposite sex."

"Just because you're antisocial doesn't mean everyone is," Kate replied, a little hurt by Cooper's remark. "I'll catch you later. And, Annie, I'll come by and pick up my stuff later if that's okay."

She left Annie and Cooper looking around the store and headed back onto the street. She was supposed to be meeting Sherrie, Jessica, and Tara in front of the Starbucks a few blocks away, so it didn't take her long to get there. When she arrived, her friends were already waiting.

"There you are," Jessica said. "We were starting to think you weren't going to show."

"I got a late start," Kate said.

"Okay," Sherrie said. "Here's the plan. We're going to hit the fabric store first to look at the costume patterns. If we don't find anything there, then we'll move on to some of the other stores and hope for the best."

"What has everyone decided on?" Tara asked.

"I talked Sean out of the Fred and Wilma Flintstone idea he had, and we're going as Rhett and Scarlett from *Gone with the Wind*," Sherrie said.

"Blair suggested that we go as Peter Pan and Wendy," said Jessica. "It's an easy costume, so I'm all for it. All I need is a nightgown."

"And Al and I are going to be Xena and Ares," said Tara. "Although I don't know where I'm going to find a breastplate around here."

"What are you and Scott going as, Kate?" Jessica asked.

"It's kind of a secret," Kate said, thinking about her Sleeping Beauty idea. "I'd rather surprise you guys the night of the dance."

"More secrets," Sherrie said, eyeing her. "You're just an enigma these days, Kate."

"At least your shadow isn't hanging around," said Tara, referring to Annie. "She gives me the creeps."

Kate ignored her and headed for the fabric shop. She went straight to the pattern books, hoping she'd find what she needed. Her mother had promised to help her put together a costume as long as she bought the pattern and material.

She was silent as she looked at the pictures in the pattern book, trying to find just the right one. Then she found it, a beautiful dress that looked just like what Princess Aurora wore in the movie. She noted the pattern number and the amount of material she would need and then shut the book.

"Time to find some satin," she said to Tara, who continued to look through the books.

Kate found the section of the store she needed and began looking at the different colors of satin. She was debating between pink and blue when Sherrie and Jessica came up holding a bolt of bright red material.

"It's *very* Scarlett, don't you think?" Sherrie asked.

"Oh, very," Kate said.

Jessica unrolled some of the cloth and Sherrie wrapped it around her shoulders. Kate laughed as Sherrie batted her eyes and did an impression of a Southern belle. Then Kate held up the two colors she was trying to choose between and listened as her friends gave their opinions of each one.

Eventually she decided on the blue material. Taking the bolt and the pattern up to the counter, she asked one of the clerks to cut it for her while she tried to hide the pattern from her friends' prying eyes.

"Not until the dance!" she said, even when they begged her to show them what she had decided on.

Afterward, the four of them stopped at a restaurant to eat. They laughed and joked as they shared an order of onion rings, pointed out guys they thought were cute at nearby tables, and picked food off each other's plates when they came. Kate was happy. It felt good to be with her old friends. There was something safe and familiar about them. She wondered

155

what Annie and Cooper were up to, though. They'd probably stayed and looked through the books from the store and found out more about Wicca. She wished she hadn't had to leave. She sighed, realizing that she wanted to be in two places at once, and she knew she couldn't be. She hoped she would never have to choose between them.

CHAPTER 12

The next afternoon, after returning from church with her parents, Kate went over to Annie's. Cooper hadn't arrived yet, so she had a few minutes to talk to Annie alone in her room.

"Do you go to church?" she asked.

"No," said Annie. "My parents weren't really into religion, and neither is my aunt. She practices Buddhist meditation, but she doesn't call herself a Buddhist. She also does yoga and all kinds of other things. She says she likes to explore different spiritualities."

"What about you?" Kate said. "What do you consider yourself?"

"Nothing, I guess," Annie answered. "I've never really gone to any one church or been part of any group. Why do you ask?"

"I was just thinking about what Sophia said yesterday about Wicca being a religion. The Goddess religion, is what she called it. I'd never thought of it as a religion before."

Annie picked up one of the books that Sophia had suggested to them. "I read some of this last night," Annie said. "It's really interesting. The woman who wrote it got into witchcraft after studying it for a class she took in college. She was raised Jewish, but after learning about Wicca she became a witch."

"But who is the Goddess?" Kate asked.

"That's kind of hard to explain," Annie said. "I think basically she's the force that created nature and everything in it."

"And what does all of this have to do with magic and spells?" Kate asked.

"Remember what Sophia said about magic being energy?" Annie said.

Kate nodded. "You said something about that when we cast a circle," she said.

"Right," said Annie. "Well, witches believe that energy comes from the natural world, and from within themselves, and that magic is learning how to use that energy to change things."

"Why do you have to worship this Goddess to be able to do that?" said Kate.

"I don't think you do," said Annie. "I mean, you and I both cast spells, and neither of us worships the Goddess."

"But our spells didn't work right," Kate said. "Maybe it's because we aren't Wiccans."

"What are you two talking about?" asked Cooper, entering the room. As she took off her coat she added, "Your aunt let me in, Annie, in case you thought I snuck in a window or something."

"We were talking about whether or not you have to be Wiccan to really do magic," said Annie.

"Lots of religions have magic," said Cooper. "Not just witchcraft."

"Like what?" asked Kate. "I've never heard of any."

"What do you call prayer?" said Cooper.

"Prayer is talking to God," Kate answered. "It's not magic."

"I know you don't call it that," said Cooper. "But think about it. What do you do when you pray? You ask God to make things happen, right?"

"Sometimes," said Kate.

"Or what about when people say prayers to the saints?" Cooper went on. "You know, like when you lose something and you pray to Saint Anthony to help you find it."

"That's not the same thing," said Kate.

"Maybe not exactly the same," said Cooper. "But it's the same principle. Isn't praying the same thing as sending your intentions out into the universe?"

"I guess doing a spell to get a better grade on a test is sort of like asking God to help out a little," said Kate doubtfully.

"And people do that every day in schools across the world," Cooper said. "But they would freak out if you told them they might be trying to do magic."

"But it's not exactly the same," said Annie. "I mean, when you do magic, you aren't asking anyone else to help you out. It's just you. And the universe."

"And God isn't the universe?" Cooper asked.

"I guess it depends on how you look at things," Annie said.

Cooper sighed. "Whatever," she said. "So, what are we going to do this afternoon?"

Kate looked at Annie. She was still trying to work out the different arguments about God and magic. What Cooper had said made sense, but Kate knew that it wasn't quite as simple as Cooper made it out to be.

"Well," Annie said. "I don't think we're quite ready to do any kind of spell to stop what Kate's and my spells have done. But I thought maybe we could try raising some energy. I read about it in one of the books I got yesterday, and it occurred to me that maybe what we need is a little practice before we move on to the big stuff."

"Fine with me," Cooper said.

"Okay," said Kate, wishing that she could be as confident about everything as Cooper seemed to be. Instead, she was feeling more and more uneasy about everything. Cooper seemed to be able to accept everything easily, and Annie was willing to consider everything and test it out, but she herself had a lot of questions. Still, they were all in this because of her, so she thought it best to go along.

"The exercise is actually pretty simple," Annie said. "We're supposed to sit holding hands and visualize ourselves filling with white light. Then we imagine passing the light to each other through our hands until we've formed a circle of light around us. Once we've done that, we picture the light moving up and forming a cone over our heads. It's called a cone of power, and it's a way of concentrating your energy and then releasing it into the universe."

"Sounds like a blast," said Cooper, seating herself in the center of the room and patting the floor with both hands.

Annie and Kate sat on either side of Cooper. Kate looked from one to the other. "How do we picture this light?" she asked.

"Just close your eyes," said Annie, taking Kate's hand.

Kate closed her fingers around Annie's. She reached out her other hand and took Cooper's hand in hers. Cooper squeezed tightly, unlike Annie's gentle pressure, but when Kate shook her hand a little Cooper eased up. They all closed their eyes.

Kate sat silently, trying to picture herself filling with light. But for some reason she was having a hard time concentrating with Cooper and Annie beside her. Her mind kept wandering, and suddenly she would realize that instead of thinking about white light she was thinking about when Scott was going to kiss her or her dress for the dance or about what she might have for dinner. Finally, after several minutes of trying to focus, she gave up.

"I can't do this," she said, opening her eyes.

"I was having a hard time, too," Annie admitted.

"Ditto," said Cooper. "It's like all of our different thoughts were interfering with each other or something."

"Maybe we need to try something else," said Annie. "I read something interesting in one of the books. It suggested raising energy by chanting. You make up a chant by doing word association."

"Word association?" said Cooper. "How's that work?"

"I say a word," Annie explained. "Then Kate says a word that my word makes her think of. Then you say a word that her word makes you think of. We keep going around the circle chanting, and as we do we let ourselves think about the images the words bring up. It's supposed to help us focus."

They joined hands again and closed their eyes. Then Annie began. "Snow," she said.

"Cold," Kate said, the word springing into her mind immediately.

"Ice," said Cooper.

"Water," Annie said after a short pause, and the second round began.

They went around, each saying a word, and the sound filled Kate's mind. "Water, Ocean, Swim, Beach, Sand, Warm, Fire, Sun, Moon, Star, Night, Black." The words flowed easily as they circled around and around. With each one, a picture flashed into Kate's mind and was quickly replaced by another as the next word was spoken. Soon she found herself sinking into a comfortable, relaxed state. And then she saw herself filled with light, and Annie and Cooper on either side of her, also filled with light.

The sound of their voices took on a new tone. It reminded Kate of bees buzzing on a warm summer day, lulling her to sleep but also filling her with excitement. She imagined the light in her body flowing out through her fingers and into Cooper's and Annie's hands. She saw it join with the light coming from their fingers, and she imagined their different lights forming one continuous ring that flowed around them like crystal-clear water.

They kept chanting, the words coming out like a song. Their voices blended together into one, and Kate imagined the words flying around their heads, carrying the light above them like butterflies. "Earth, flower, bloom," she heard them say.

The light rose up, and Kate pictured it coming to a point. The words grew louder. "Wind, fly, bird," they chanted. "Feather, float, dream."

Cooper squeezed Kate's hand, and Kate squeezed Annie's. It was as if they were signaling one another. They lifted their joined hands up into the air. "Mother, child, birth," they said, and let the last word hang in the air as they stopped chanting.

Kate's heart was beating fiercely in her chest.

She could feel the blood moving through her body. She could feel Annie's and Cooper's hands in hers, and it was almost like they shared the same blood. She'd never felt anything like it. It was as if the whole room were filled with light, and they were at the center of it.

Kate opened her eyes. Annie and Cooper had also opened theirs, and they all looked around at one another.

"Did we do it?" Kate asked.

"I think so," said Annie.

"I'm really hungry all of a sudden," said Cooper. "Do you have anything to eat?"

Oddly enough, they all felt hungry. Going downstairs, they searched the kitchen for food and returned to Annie's room carrying bags of chips and things to drink. Sitting on the floor, they ate and talked about what they'd just done.

"That was amazing," Annie said. "I could really feel something moving inside me."

"I felt a little of that when I did my own ritual," Kate said. "But it was nothing like what we did."

"The chanting really helped," said Cooper. "But why are we so hungry?"

Annie picked up one of the books she'd gotten at the bookstore and opened it. "I think I saw something about that in here when I was reading," she said, leafing through the pages. "Here it is. 'After raising and releasing energy, you may feel a sense of exhilaration,'" she read. "'You may even feel lightheaded or slightly dizzy. It's important after doing this kind of energy work to eat and drink something. This helps reconnect you with your body and with the earth, and it allows any excess energy you've raised to be reabsorbed. This process is called grounding.'"

"Grounding," said Cooper, taking a handful of chips. "Like when you work with electricity. You always have a ground wire to channel the electrical current so it doesn't run wild and do damage. I learned that when I rewired my guitar amp."

"I just hope we didn't bother your aunt with all the chanting," Kate said.

"Don't worry about that," Annie told her. "You can't hear much downstairs. Besides, I don't think we were that loud."

"I wish we'd written down the words to the chant," Kate said. "I don't really remember them."

"Maybe that's part of the magic," Cooper suggested. "If you did the same chant all the time, it wouldn't be spontaneous. I think one of the reasons it was so powerful was because it came from the moment. You know, like when you make up poetry on the spot. It has an edge to it."

"I'll have to take your word for that one," Kate said. "I'm not really an on-the-spot poet."

"What about cheers at basketball games?" said Annie. "That's kind of the same thing."

Kate thought about it. Annie was right. She always liked it when the crowd started doing cheers at the games. It lifted her spirits and made her feel like she could do anything. The pounding of their feet, the clapping, and the sound of hundreds of voices working together had a special effect on her.

"As long as we don't have to have cheerleaders," Cooper said. "Those ditzes make me sick with their pom-poms and their little skirts."

Cooper's description of the cheerleaders made Kate think of Sherrie. She pictured her friend leading cheers at one of the guys' games. Sherrie was really good at it. She loved to come up with new chants and new routines to get the crowd into the game. But what would she think of the chant that Kate, Annie, and Cooper had just done? Would she think it was cool, the way she thought a new cheer was cool? Would she see raising the energy level at a ball game the same way she would see raising energy in a magical circle? Kate knew that she wouldn't, and that bothered her.

"I've got to get home," she said suddenly. "I have a lot of homework to do before tomorrow."

"I guess I should do some work, too," Annie said reluctantly.

"What about planning a ritual?" Cooper asked. "Shouldn't we talk about what we're going to do to fix the things Kate started? I thought that was the whole point of getting together in the first place."

"I think maybe we need some more practice," said Kate, gathering up her things. "Can we talk about it later?"

Cooper shrugged. "It's your life," she said.

As Kate walked home, her mood worsened. She'd felt so happy and powerful sitting in the circle with Annie and Cooper. But that was only one part of her life. The rest of her time centered around being on the team, trying to be a normal high school student, and, she hoped, being Scott's girlfriend. If she kept practicing Wicca, she wouldn't be able to keep what she was doing a secret forever, and she knew her friends would never understand her involvement in something like witchcraft. She wasn't even sure she believed a lot of the things that witches seemed to believe. Sure, it had been fun raising energy, but she wasn't sure how all the new beliefs sat with her. Annie and Cooper seemed to be able to accept things so easily, but Kate wasn't sure she could do the same thing.

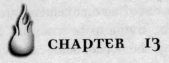

CHAPTER 13

That night, while she was working on an English assignment, Scott called her to tell her that he'd cobbled together his Prince Phillip costume for the Valentine's Day dance and to ask her what color her dress was going to be. "I want to make sure the flowers I get are exactly right," he said.

When Kate hung up, she started thinking about the dance and about Scott. She knew that witchcraft had had a lot to do with why he had asked her out. Now that she knew a little more about how magic worked, that made her uneasy. But what made her even more uneasy was the thought that, even if he liked her for who she was, Scott probably wouldn't want a girlfriend who practiced Wicca. He probably didn't even know what Wicca was.

And she knew that Scott wouldn't be the only boy who didn't know anything about witchcraft. How would she ever have a normal social life if she remained involved in Wicca? She imagined trying to explain to a guy that she couldn't go out with him on a Friday night because she and her friends had to raise energy or cast a spell. He'd think she was out of her mind.

The more she thought about it, the more she realized that Wicca was just a little too weird for her. She wasn't like Sophia, with her Indian print clothes and her funny store. She wasn't like Annie, who would rather sit up in her room reading than hang out with other kids. And she definitely wasn't like Cooper, who didn't seem to care whether anyone liked her or not. She was plain old Kate Morgan, with a normal family and a normal life. She just wanted to fit in. And becoming a witch was not going to help her do that.

Maybe, she thought, the problem wasn't that the spell she'd cast was out of control. Maybe the real problem was that she wasn't letting it run its course. Things did seem to be calming down a little. Her friends were hanging out with her. Scott was still interested. Sure, people were mad at Annie about Terri's accident, but they'd forget about that eventually. And it wasn't like Annie had been popular before anyway. She wouldn't care if people thought she was kind of weird. Maybe the best thing was to just let everything settle down on its own. Maybe doing more spells would just stir up the energy again and cause more bad things to happen.

The more she thought about it, the more Kate became convinced that this was the best way to go. By the time she turned out the light and went to bed, she'd decided that maybe she didn't need to ever do another ritual. Now she just had to tell Cooper and Annie.

She got her chance first thing the next morning when she arrived at school. She spotted Cooper and Annie near the entrance, talking, as she approached.

"Hey," Annie said, smiling. "Cooper and I were just talking about what kind of ritual we should do. We had this idea that—"

"I need to talk to you about that," Kate said, interrupting Annie before she could get started. "I don't think we really need to do another ritual."

Annie looked at Cooper with a puzzled expression. "What do you mean?" she asked Kate.

Kate looked around to see who might be watching them. She didn't want too many people to see her talking to Cooper and Annie, especially Annie.

"I just don't think we need to do any more spells," she said.

"But what about stopping what's going on?" Annie asked.

Kate suddenly felt uncomfortable. Her plan had seemed so sensible the night before. But now, facing Annie and Cooper, she wasn't so sure. Part of her wanted to talk about magic and plan another ritual, but she also wanted to put it all behind her.

"Things don't feel so bad right now, that's all," Kate said. She couldn't explain how she felt to

Annie. Annie had never been part of the in crowd. She wouldn't understand.

"Maybe not for you," Cooper said. "But what about for Annie? And what about for everyone else whose lives have been affected by what you did?"

"Could you keep it down?" Kate said. Several people had heard Cooper's raised voice and turned to look at them.

"Cooper's right," said Annie. "Maybe things are calming down for you, but that doesn't mean everything is fine. We can't just have your spell turning things upside down forever."

"It won't be forever," Kate said. "Things are already getting back to normal. Not even one guy has said hello to me this morning."

As if on cue, a boy passing by turned to Kate and smiled. "Hi, Kate," he said. "You've got my vote for queen."

"Oh, yeah," said Cooper. "Things are all perfectly normal. What's gotten into you, Kate? Yesterday you were all into this, and today you're saying you don't want to do it anymore."

"All I said was that I don't think we need to do another ritual right now," said Kate.

"When then?" asked Annie. "After the dance, when you don't need to have Scott around to be your date? After the next chemistry test, when you don't need to do well? I guess we'll just wait until it's convenient for you."

Kate was shocked that Annie would say those

things to her. "You know I didn't mean for any of this to happen," she said.

"I know that," said Annie. "But now you don't seem to be in any big hurry to stop it." She paused for a moment, waiting for Kate to say something. When she didn't, Annie continued. "Remember when I said that Cooper was afraid of magic?" she said. "I was wrong. You're the one who's afraid, Kate. You're afraid of things changing."

"Maybe I am," Kate said. "But I have a lot more to lose than the two of you do."

There was a shocked silence as Cooper and Annie stared at Kate. Nothing was going the way Kate had planned it. She thought that maybe Cooper and Annie would understand. But just as Sherrie, Jessica, and Tara would never understand her interest in witchcraft, she knew that Annie and Cooper would never understand her wanting to have a normal life. She wanted to make them see what she was going through, but she didn't know how.

"Look," she said finally. "Can we talk about this later? This isn't the best place for this conversation."

"Right," said Cooper, her eyes flashing. "You might be seen talking to someone your friends wouldn't approve of."

Kate opened her mouth to argue, but at that moment Tara, Sherrie, and Jessica really did come around the corner. When they saw Kate standing with Annie and Cooper, they stopped.

"I see your biggest fan is back," Sherrie said, sneering at Annie. "What does she want this time, an autograph?"

Tara and Jessica snickered at Sherrie's joke. Annie turned bright red and looked at the floor.

"Don't you three have somewhere else to be?" Cooper said.

"What are you, her keeper?" asked Sherrie.

"Her friend," said Cooper.

"You'd better watch out, Sher," said Jessica. "They might push you down some stairs too if you're not careful."

Sherrie looked at Kate. "Is there a problem here?" she said.

Kate looked at Annie and Cooper. Annie seemed ready to burst into tears, and Cooper was staring at Kate angrily.

"Yeah, Kate, tell us—is there a problem here?" Cooper said.

Kate knew Cooper was challenging her. So was Sherrie. They both wanted her to choose which side she was on. It wasn't fair. She wanted to be friends with everyone, but they wouldn't let her, and she felt trapped in the middle. Her mind raced with thoughts as she tried to come up with some way out of the situation. But she knew there was only one way. She had to pick.

"No," she said. "There's no problem." She looked over at Sherrie. "I was just telling them that I wouldn't be able to join them for lunch."

Sherrie tossed her head triumphantly. Annie burst into tears and ran off. Cooper looked at Kate with disgust and then turned away to go after Annie. Kate wanted to run after both of them and try to explain why she'd had to do what she'd done. But her old friends were already sweeping her down the hallway.

"That was a good one," Tara said. "Did they really ask you to have lunch with them?"

"Wasn't that Cooper Rivers?" asked Jessica. "That girl is a serious sociopath. Who does she think she is with that pink hair?"

"She and the Crandall chick are a perfect pair," said Sherrie. "They can form their own freak show."

Kate didn't say a word. She felt miserable, turning on Annie and Cooper like that. But she hadn't had a choice. She'd been friends with Sherrie, Jessica, and Tara way longer. Besides, Kate had much more in common with them than she did with Cooper and Annie. They'd just been thrown together because of a bad situation. She liked them, but when it came down to it, she couldn't see them being the same tight group that she and her other friends were.

In chemistry she tried to catch Annie's eye as she walked by her seat, but Annie kept her head in her notebook and didn't even look up. She didn't even volunteer when Miss Blackwood asked for someone to help out with an experiment she was doing. Kate had never known Annie to be so silent in chemistry class, and she knew it was because her feelings were hurt.

Despite feeling bad about what she'd done to Annie and Cooper that morning, Kate had to admit that things did appear to be more normal. No one else seemed to be angry with her. Scott walked her to several classes, and at lunch everyone joked around and gossiped like they usually did. By the time the end of the day rolled around, Kate was convinced that the magic had settled down once and for all. More and more she was sure that she'd made the right choice. And although Annie and Cooper might be disappointed, Kate thought she might still be able to repair her friendship with them. They could never be the same kind of friends that Sherrie, Jessica, and Tara were. They just needed time to calm down, she told herself. Then they would see that it was all for the best.

She was walking home, thinking about the work she had to do on her Valentine's Day dance costume that night, when she heard someone running behind her. She turned and saw Cooper coming toward her. Her breath formed clouds in the frosty air, and her cheeks were red.

"I need to talk to you," she said.

Kate looked around.

"Don't worry," Cooper said. "Your friends aren't here. I made sure of that before I followed you."

"I wasn't—"

"Yes, you were," Cooper said. "But I'm not here to talk about them."

"Then what do you want to talk about?" Kate asked.

"Annie was right when she said I was scared of witchcraft," Cooper said.

"That's what you had to tell me?" Kate said. "You ran after me for that?"

"No," said Cooper. "I ran after you to tell you why I was scared. Why I *am* scared."

"I don't think I want to hear this," Kate said.

"Why?" said Cooper. "Are you afraid you might hear something you can relate to?"

They stood on the sidewalk, neither speaking. Kate wanted to go home, but she couldn't. She knew it had taken a lot for Cooper to come after her.

"Remember how I told you that magic runs in my family?" Cooper said.

Kate nodded. "I didn't know what you meant," she said. "And you didn't seem to want to talk about it."

"My grandmother was a witch," said Cooper. "She probably wouldn't have called herself that, but it's what she was. She came here from Scotland. When I was little, she used to tell me stories about fairies and goblins and stuff like that. My mother hated it when she did that, but I loved it. And sometimes she would play these little games with me. At least I thought they were games for a long time.

Now I know they were magical exercises."

"What kind of exercises?" Kate asked. Cooper had never revealed so much about herself before, and Kate was intrigued.

"She would have me close my eyes and imagine different things," Cooper said. "Different places. Different people. She would talk to me softly and teach me little rhymes. I always thought it was just make-believe, but she was really trying to teach me to focus my thoughts. When I got older, she taught me some basic spells—protection spells she'd learned from her mother and things like that. She didn't call them spells. She just said that everyone knew them where she came from."

"Why did that make you afraid of Wicca?" Kate said.

"Once I asked my mother about all the things my grandmother was teaching me," Cooper said. "She got really angry, and she yelled at my grandmother. They had a huge fight. My mother told her not to fill my mind with superstitious nonsense. My grandmother cried and was really sad. She thought she'd done something bad. No matter how much I asked her to, she wouldn't tell me any more stories or teach me any more of her secrets. Worst of all, she and my mother barely spoke for the next couple of years, and my grandmother died before they could patch things up."

"You didn't make her die," Kate said.

"I know," said Cooper. "But in a way I felt

responsible for their fight. And I also blamed witch-craft. I thought that if my grandmother had just been normal, like everyone else's grandmother, she wouldn't have had the fight with my mother and maybe she wouldn't have died with them not talking. I also saw how embarrassed my mother was by her mother, and how she totally rejected everything my grandmother tried to share with her. She wanted a normal mother, and she didn't get one, so she tried to make her normal by pretending and by fighting. But it didn't work."

"I'm not pretending to be something I'm not," Kate said. "I'm not a witch."

"Maybe not," said Cooper. "But you're never going to find out who or what you are if you keep running from something because you're afraid it doesn't make you what everyone else is. You're like my mother was. You're afraid of being different."

"I'm sorry I hurt your feelings this morning," Kate said. "And I'm sorry about your grandmother. But I still don't think doing more magic is going to change anything."

"Annie's the one you should apologize to," Cooper said. "She thought you were her friend."

Kate was silent.

"Stop trying to be like everyone else," Cooper persisted. "You felt what we did the other night. That was real. There's something in you that needs to get out, and if you keep bottling it up you're going to explode."

Kate sighed. Cooper was giving her a chance to change her mind. But was she ready to do that? Was she ready to not care about what people thought of her? Was she ready to find out if she was really a witch?

She looked at Cooper. "I've got to go," she said. "Tell Annie I'm sorry."

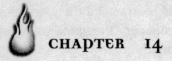

CHAPTER 14

When Kate got home, she discovered that her mother had spent the day sewing her costume for the dance. It was almost done, and it was hanging on the back of Kate's door with a note telling her to try it on so that they could make whatever adjustments were necessary when her mother came home from the party she was catering.

Kate took the dress from the hanger and pulled it over her head. It fluttered down around her in soft waves. It fit perfectly, and as Kate stood in front of the mirror looking at herself she really did feel like a princess from a fairy tale. She couldn't wait until Saturday night, when everyone would see her in her costume and she and Scott would dance together. Maybe she would even be elected Valentine's Day queen. She had been upset when Scott first showed her the posters, but now it didn't seem like such a bad idea. In fact, she sort of hoped she would win. It would be the perfect ending to the evening.

She removed the dress and hung it back up. Then she sat down to do some homework. But as she worked, she kept thinking about Annie. Kate really hadn't meant to hurt Annie's feelings, but she knew she had. Annie had been a good friend to her. Kate hated to think about her being sad. And Cooper's words kept running through her head, making her feel even worse. Partly because she felt so badly about Cooper and Annie, and partly because, deep down, she knew she was responsible for all the mayhem of the last several days, she decided to get some help, and she knew exactly where to go.

She grabbed her jacket and headed for the door. It was still early. If she hurried, she could get to Crones' Circle and back before her mother came home and wondered where she was.

When she reached the shop, it was just starting to get dark. There was a light on inside the store, and the window shone invitingly. Kate pushed open the door and went in. The same gray cat was sitting on the counter, but there was no sign of Sophia. Then someone emerged from the back of the store. It was another woman, thin and elfin looking. She had short, brown hair and dark eyes, and she was dressed in a soft peach-colored sweater and faded jeans.

"Is Sophia here?" Kate asked.

"I'm afraid not," the woman said, regarding Kate with interest. "It's her day off. Can I help you with anything? I'm Archer."

"My friends and I were in here on Saturday," Kate said. "Sophia helped us pick out some books."

Archer smiled. "Yes, she told me about you," she said. "She said that you had lots of questions."

"I had a few more I was hoping she could help me with," Kate said.

"Well, maybe I can answer them," suggested Archer. "Are they about witchcraft or something else?"

"Witchcraft," Kate replied nervously. "Are you a witch, too?"

"Yes," said Archer. When Kate didn't respond, she added, "Why don't you come in back and we can talk. I was just making some tea."

Kate was relieved that Archer seemed to understand her nervousness. She didn't really know what she wanted to ask, but she knew she needed some advice. She followed Archer through the curtain that hung behind the counter and found herself in a small room. A little table sat in the center, covered with a red cloth. Several candles were burning on it, and the room was filled with the scent of vanilla. Two comfortable-looking armchairs, covered in dark green velvet, were arranged on opposite sides of the table.

"This is where we do Tarot readings," said Archer. "I don't have any appointments tonight, though, so tonight it's just the tea table."

She motioned for Kate to take one of the chairs, then went through a doorway and returned a moment later with a kettle and two mugs. She poured water into the mugs and the smell of mint rose with the steam.

"I hope you like mint," Archer said. "I find it makes these winter nights a little less frigid."

Kate took the mug and held it in her hands, breathing in the mint. It did make her feel better. So did being in such a cozy room. She took a sip of the tea and felt it warming her as it went down.

"What is it you have questions about?" Archer asked as she sat down.

"You said you do Tarot readings," Kate said, hesitating. "Could you maybe do one for me?" She hadn't even thought about having a Tarot reading before Archer had mentioned it, but suddenly it seemed like a good idea.

Archer reached behind her and took something from a shelf. It was a box wrapped in a scarlet silk scarf. Archer untied the knotted scarf and pulled the top off the box. She turned it upside down and a stack of cards fell into her hand. Kate saw that each one had a different picture on it.

"Have you ever had a Tarot reading before?" Archer asked.

Kate shook her head. "I've seen the cards before," she said. "At least I've seen them in the boxes. But I never knew exactly how they were used."

"We use them as a divination tool," Archer said.

"You mean to see the future?" said Kate.

"Not exactly," Archer explained. "They show

what the circumstances around a situation are and what might happen if the person asking the question acts in certain ways. Would you like me to show you?"

Kate nodded. Archer took the cards and sifted through them. She picked one out and put it in the center of the table. The card depicted a young person holding a sword.

"That's the Page of Swords," Archer said. "It represents a young woman or man like you. So think of that card as representing you."

She took the remaining cards and shuffled them several times. Then she divided them into three piles on the table. "Now, choose a pile," she said to Kate.

Kate picked the middle pile, and Archer put it on top of the other two. Then she picked up the first card and turned it over, laying it over the Page of Swords. The picture on the card showed an angel blowing a trumpet.

"Judgment," Archer said. "It's a powerful card. It represents a shift in consciousness. Have you been doing a lot of thinking about spiritual things lately?"

Kate nodded. Archer turned over the next card and laid it crosswise over the angel card. This card showed an unhappy-looking man sitting in front of three wooden cups. A hand holding another cup reached out from a cloud over his head, but he didn't seem to see it.

"What does that mean?" Kate asked. For some reason, the image troubled her.

"The Four of Cups," said Archer. "It suggests that you're bored with things and want them to change, but that perhaps you're hesitant about making the changes you need to."

Kate didn't say anything. It was strange that Archer could tell so many things about her that were true just from looking at the cards. She *had* been thinking about spiritual things a lot lately, and she was definitely hesitant about making changes in her life. She wondered what would come next.

Archer laid out four more cards, placing them around the center cards. She looked at the arrangement for a moment. "You've had to make some difficult choices lately, haven't you?" she asked. "And some things have been happening that haven't been very easy to deal with, although some of them have been good."

Kate thought about everything that had been going on. She'd certainly gotten a lot of the things she'd asked for, but they hadn't turned out the way she'd wanted them to. And a lot of good things *had* happened, like meeting Annie and Cooper, but she didn't know how to make them fit into the rest of her life.

"It's been a rough week or so," she admitted. "All kinds of things have been going on, and I'm not sure what any of it means."

"You're unsure of what to do," said Archer. "Part

of you wants one thing, but another part is afraid to let go and make the changes that would let you have that thing you want."

"How do you know all that?" Kate asked, a little freaked out that her life seemed to be such an open book.

Archer pointed to the cards one at a time. "The Ace of Cups," she said, indicating the card at the top of the arrangement. It showed a sun rising out of a cup. "It suggests that what you really want is to be happy, to experience the joy of living a full life. But then there's the Five of Cups beneath you." She tapped the card at the bottom of the arrangement, which had an image of a figure looking at three cups that had spilled on the ground. Two other cups sat behind the figure, unnoticed. "That card indicates that you recently got something you thought you wanted, but that you lost something else in the process."

The spells, Kate thought to herself. She certainly had gotten something that she'd thought she wanted, but it had caused a lot of problems. And every time she had to make a choice between two things, she seemed to make the wrong one. Looking at the Five of Cups, she suddenly thought that the three spilled cups reminded her of her friendship with Jessica, Tara, and Sherrie, while the two full cups made her think of Annie and Cooper. But what that all meant, she didn't know.

"These other two cards indicate things that have

recently happened and things that might happen in the near future," Archer continued. "This card is the Tower. See how the lightning is hitting the top of it and it seems to be on fire?"

Kate looked at the card. It made her feel nervous. There was something ominous about it. "Is it bad?" she asked.

"None of the cards are necessarily bad," Archer answered. "They simply represent influences that are affecting a situation. This card tells me that you've probably recently experienced some dramatic change in your life. Something that made you rethink a lot of what you thought was true. And this card," she said, picking up a card showing two people holding one another, "shows me that whatever happened to you is forcing you to choose between two very powerful things. This is the Lovers. They represent having to decide between opposing forces."

That was something Kate could definitely relate to. She was feeling pulled in many different directions: between her old friends and her new ones, between fitting in and being different. The card also made her think of Scott, and how she was glad they were together but couldn't help feeling a little guilty about how it had come to be.

"How do I make these decisions?" she asked Archer.

"The cards don't tell you what to do," Archer said. "They just tell you what might happen if you do certain tnings or don't do them. Let's look at the last four."

She took the remaining cards and arranged them in a straight line up one side of the table, almost like a ladder. The bottom one showed a woman tied with ropes and blindfolded. Eight swords surrounded her, stuck into the ground.

"She looks like a prisoner," Kate said.

"She is," said Archer. "She can't make up her mind. She feels trapped by her circumstances and doesn't know how to get free."

"Who is she?" Kate asked. As she looked at the bound woman, she felt really sorry for her.

"She's you," said Archer. "This card represents how you feel about your situation."

Kate stared at the card. *That's me,* she thought sadly. *I do feel trapped by all of this and I don't know how to get free.* She hoped the answer would be found in the rest of the cards.

"And who is that?" she asked, looking at the next card. It depicted a young person holding a cup. A fish was leaping up from the water in the cup. "Is that me, too?"

"The Page of Cups," Archer told her. "It usually represents an artistic young person who is trying to help you. Does that sound like anyone in your life?"

Annie, Kate thought instantly, *or maybe even Cooper.* Both of them fit the description, but in different ways. "I think I know who it is," she told

Archer. "Does that mean she's important in all of this?"

"She could be," Archer said. "It depends on whether or not you let her help you."

The next card was a picture of a man hanging upside down from a tree. His foot was tied to one of the branches, and his hands were behind his back.

"Is he dead?" Kate asked, hoping the card didn't signify something she didn't want to hear. She was still thinking about how Archer had suggested that she needed the person represented by the Page of Cups to help her. Annie and Cooper had both offered to do that, and she'd turned them down. She hoped she hadn't made a terrible mistake.

"No," said Archer. "But he symbolizes a kind of death. He's the Hanged Man, and he represents letting go of old ideas and ways of thinking in order to move forward in life. The card appearing here suggests that you want to move forward but are having trouble doing that."

"And what's this last card?" said Kate. She picked up the final card and looked at it. It was a beautiful picture of three young women holding cups. They seemed to be toasting one another, and they were smiling and happy. Behind them a giant yellow flower was opening up.

"The Three of Cups," said Archer. "One of my favorite cards. It represents the perfection of friendship and the beginning of something very special."

"Is that what's going to happen then?" asked Kate hopefully. It didn't seem like a bad card to end with to her.

"It could," said Archer. "But only if you make it happen. It seems there are some things standing in your way. You're going to have to make some difficult choices if you really want to achieve what the Three of Cups represents."

Kate looked at all of the cards. She'd never seen any of them before, but as she looked at them all laid out she could almost understand the story they told. She knew it was a story about her and about what she was going through and needed to do. But she didn't know if she'd be able to do it.

"Thanks for doing that," she said to Archer, who was gathering up the cards and putting them back in their box.

"It's my pleasure," she said. "I hope it helped some."

"It did," Kate said. "I have a lot to think about now."

Archer sat back in her chair and drank some of her tea. "What was it you wanted to ask Sophia?" she said.

Pouring out the whole, sad story took some time, and when Kate looked up at the wall and noticed the hour on the clock, she realized more time had passed than she had thought. Her mother would be home soon, and she had to go.

"Thanks again for the Tarot card reading," Kate said as she stood up and put on her jacket.

Archer followed Kate back into the main part of the store. She opened a drawer and pulled something out, then handed it to Kate. It was a card printed with the picture from the Three of Cups.

"Take this with you," Archer said. "It might help remind you of your reading and of what you need to do."

Kate took the card and looked at the faces of the three women on it. Their eyes looked into hers. "Thanks," she said as she slipped the card into her pocket. "And I think I know what my next step has to be."

CHAPTER 15

The next morning Kate got to school early and went looking for Cooper and Annie. She couldn't find Annie, but she found Cooper in the music room.

"You were right," she said.

"About what?" Cooper responded.

"About everything," Kate said. "About my being afraid. About my friends. I am scared."

"And what are you going to do about that?" asked Cooper.

"I'm not really sure yet," Kate said. "But I know what I'm going to do first. What *we* are going to do first. A ritual. Tomorrow night. It's the full moon. That's supposed to be good for doing magic, right?"

Cooper shook her head. "You're really something else," she said. "One minute you pretend you don't know me and let your friend take the blame for something you caused, and the next you come around all filled with plans for doing a ritual. Do you expect me to be all happy about this? And what about Annie? Do you think she's really going to want to do something to help you after everything you've done?"

Kate didn't know what to say. All night she'd been thinking about her plan, and it hadn't gone anything like this. The Tarot cards seemed to be telling her that she needed to get back together with Annie and Cooper.

"I haven't talked to Annie about it yet," Kate admitted. "I haven't seen her."

"That's because she's not coming to school," Cooper said.

"What do you mean?" Kate asked. "Is she sick?"

"She was suspended," Cooper said. "The school called last night and told her that they'd decided to hold a disciplinary hearing. Apparently Terri's parents decided to make a stink. And until this is settled, Annie's out of here."

"But she didn't do anything!" Kate protested.

"Try telling that to them," Cooper said. "Or maybe you'd just rather keep your mouth shut and stay out of trouble yourself."

Kate started to speak but Cooper was walking away from her down the hall and not looking back.

Kate ran after her. "Come on, Cooper," she said. "I said I was sorry. I said I wanted to do another ritual. What else do I have to do to convince you that I'm serious?"

Cooper stopped in the middle of the hall and turned to face Kate. "You know what I want you to do?" she said. "I want you to stay away from me. Fix your own problems, and leave me out of it. I don't need your stupid little friends looking down their noses at me. I don't need you talking to me only when it's convenient or when you need something. I don't need any of it."

She stormed off, leaving Kate standing alone in the hallway. Kate looked around and saw that one of her Valentine's Day queen posters was staring back at her. Her smiling face seemed to mock her, laughing stupidly. Looking at it made Kate furious, and she ran up and snatched it from the wall. Ripping it in half, she threw the pieces on the floor. Then she ran to another one hanging farther down the hall and ripped that one off the wall, too.

She found herself running through the school, looking for pictures of herself and tearing them down. Tears of frustration streamed down her cheeks as she sought out every last poster and ripped them to pieces. As she destroyed each one, she felt herself letting go of something inside. It was like each piece of paper she tore off was a piece of the unhappiness that had been building up in her ever since things began to go wrong.

When she found the last poster and destroyed it, she knew what she had to do next. Getting her things from her locker, she ran out the front doors and down the street. She didn't care that she was skipping school. She didn't care that she might get into trouble. She had something more important to do.

She ran until she got to Annie's house, where she held the buzzer down until she heard someone coming. When the door opened and she saw Annie standing inside, she started crying again.

"Oh, Annie," she said. "I'm so sorry for everything. I'm sorry about asking for your help and then hurting your feelings. I'm sorry about letting you take the blame for me and not standing up for you. I'm sorry about pretending to not know you. I'm sorry about it all. Can you please forgive me?" She was sobbing now, and she knew she must look awful.

"Come inside," said Annie. "You'll catch cold standing there like that."

Kate went in, and Annie shut the door.

"I'm sorry for coming over like this," Kate said. She was afraid that if she stopped talking Annie would tell her to go away. "But after Archer did the Tarot card reading and Cooper yelled at me and—"

"Slow down," Annie said. "Who's Archer? And what Tarot card reading?"

Kate tried to stop crying. She wiped her eyes on her coat sleeve and then remembered the card in her pocket. She took it out and showed it to Annie.

"See," she said. "It's you and me and Cooper. It's what's supposed to happen. But I was afraid of letting it happen. I still am, I guess. But I know we have to do a ritual. At least one more, to make everything okay again."

"I think you should start at the beginning,"

Annie said, looking at the card. "This sounds like a good story."

She and Kate went up to her room and sat down. Kate began by telling Annie how Cooper had chased after her the day before, and how she'd then gone to Crones' Circle and talked to Archer.

"I really can't tell you how sorry I am about everything," Kate said. "I don't expect you to understand or to forgive me. I know I acted like a real jerk."

"I can't argue with that," Annie said. "But I do sort of understand. Believe me, I know what it's like to have people think you're weird."

"But you're not weird," Kate said, taking Annie's hand. "You're really great. I can't imagine anyone else who would still talk to me after all of this. Cooper sure won't."

"Let me talk to her," Annie said. "But you still haven't told me what your big plan is for this ritual."

Kate told Annie about the ritual she had thought of the night before. When she was done, she looked at Annie expectantly. "So, what do you think?"

"I think it sounds great," said Annie. "How did you think of it?"

"I was looking at the card Archer gave me and thinking about my Tarot reading," Kate said. "And suddenly I had this vision of what we could do. Do you think it will work?"

"Has anything else we've tried?" said Annie. "It

can't hurt. And what better night to do it than on the full moon."

"Then you'll talk to Cooper and try to get her to come?" asked Kate.

Annie promised to try. Then Kate walked back to school, sneaking in just in time to get to her art class. As she worked on the painting she was doing, she thought more about the ritual she had in mind. She hoped that Cooper would agree to participate. But she couldn't worry about that. She and Annie could do it alone if they really had to. Either way, she had a lot of planning to do so she would be ready.

After school she went home and got to work. Going into her mother's sewing room, she opened the big trunk that contained all the material her mother used for her various projects. Kate looked through the different pieces of cloth and selected three that she really liked. One was a dark blue, another forest green, and the third a rich purple. She took the material and laid it out on the table her mother used for cutting out patterns. Then she got out the scissors and went to work.

A couple of hours later she was finished. She looked at her handiwork and was satisfied. The robes weren't perfect, but they would do. She cleaned up the bits of cloth and pieces of thread and folded the robes. Then she went into her room, took out a notebook, and began to write.

When she finally went to bed that night, she

was exhausted and happy. Now, if Annie had done her part everything would be okay. She would know in the morning.

Wednesday dawned clear and cold. When Kate looked out her window she saw a pure blue winter sky without a cloud in it. She hoped it would be the same way that evening.

While she was at her locker, Cooper approached her. "All right," she said. "I'm in. Annie called last night and said the two of you made all nice and I shouldn't be pissed off at you anymore. She also said you had some great idea. Want to let me in on it?"

"Just be at Ryder Beach tonight," Kate said.

"The beach?" Cooper said. "Are you nuts? It will be freezing."

"I know," said Kate. "But be there anyway. Do you know the little cove past the rocks at the far end of the beach?"

"Yeah," said Cooper. "I go there to work on songs sometimes."

"Meet us there at eight," Kate said. "Here's what you need to bring." She handed Cooper a list.

"Okay," said Cooper after scanning the list. "It's your party."

"See you at eight," Kate said.

The rest of the day crawled by as Kate waited for the time when she could go home and get ready. She also had to get through basketball practice, so it was after six when she got home. She barely said a word during dinner as she wolfed down the lasagna her mother had made.

"What's the rush?" her father asked as she cleared her plate.

"I'm going to Tara's house to study," Kate said. "We have a big test tomorrow, and I need to go over a lot of stuff." She felt bad about making up a story, but it was partly true. They *were* having another quiz in chemistry, and she *was* going to see her friends, just not Tara. And she wouldn't be doing any studying.

In her room, she packed a backpack with the things she needed. Going into her closet, she took out the box containing the candles and the Ken doll. She put everything into the backpack, along with the robes she'd made and her notebook. Then she went downstairs, said good-bye to her parents, and left the house.

She took the bus through town to the waterfront area and got off. Going down the long wooden steps that led to Ryder Beach, she walked along the shore to the far end. The wind coming off of the ocean was cold, but Kate felt a growing sense of excitement as she climbed over the rocks that separated the little cove from the rest of the stretch of sand. The cove was protected by the rock walls that surrounded it on all sides, so it was less windy there. Plus, no one would be able to see them unless they crossed the rocks, and it was unlikely that anyone would do that on a February night.

Annie and Cooper hadn't arrived yet, so Kate began preparing the space by herself. She took a piece of driftwood and used it to draw a circle in the sand. She drew it far enough away from the water that the waves wouldn't erase it as they darted up the beach and retreated again. Then she took the small candles from her pack and set them in the sand around the circle. She was putting the last one in when Annie appeared, walking over the rocks.

"It took me longer than I thought to get here," she said, setting down a bag. "But I brought everything you asked for."

"Great," said Kate. "I need more candles." She opened the bag and took out the candles she'd asked Annie to get. She pushed the glass holders into the sand around the rest of the edge of the circle. Then she opened a box of matches and started lighting them. When she was done, a circle of light filled the cove, casting shadows on the sand and the surrounding rocks.

"Now help me make a smaller circle of stones in the center of the big circle," Kate told Annie.

They gathered up a number of rocks from around the cove and placed them in the center of the circle. Kate dug a hole in the sand and placed the rocks around it, making a small fire pit. Then she and Annie got some pieces of driftwood and piled them in the ring of rocks. Kate balled up some newspapers she'd brought with her and tucked them beneath the wood. She lit the paper and watched as the flames licked the wood and it started to burn.

"I didn't know you were a Girl Scout," she heard Cooper say as she climbed over the rocks and entered the cove. She was carrying three balloons tied to strings, and they bounced around as she walked.

"It's one of the bonuses of having a dad who owns a sporting goods store," Kate answered. "You should see me pitch a tent."

"Well, this is certainly cozy," Cooper said, looking around. "At least as cozy as it gets on a winter night on a beach. Where do you want these? It took a lot of doing to keep them from flying away on the way here, I'll have you know. I don't see why you couldn't have asked for plain old balloons."

"I'll take those," said Kate.

Cooper handed her the balloons, and Kate wrapped the strings around a stick, which she stuck in the sand. Then she took the robes she'd made out of her backpack and handed them to Cooper and Annie. "I made them big so they'd go over our jackets," she said as they pulled them on.

"Very witchy," said Annie, spinning around in the green robe.

"How come I got purple?" Cooper asked.

"It goes with your hair," Kate teased, flapping the sleeves of her blue robe like some kind of raven. She looked around. Everything was ready. It was time to begin. She motioned for Cooper and Annie to join her inside the circle of candles. They stood at different points in the circle, looking at each other across the fire that was crackling in the center. Above them, the full moon shone brightly in the black sky, its reflection floating on the waves like a giant, pale stone.

"Let's cast the circle," Annie said. She and Kate had already planned that part of the ritual, and one of the things that Kate had put on Cooper's list was a request that she call one of the directions.

Cooper turned to the east and raised her arms high over her head. "East!" she called out dramatically. "Creature of air. Come join us in our circle, and bring with you the inspiration of the wind."

As if hearing her call, a breeze moved through the cove, making their robes billow out and chilling their faces with its touch. *This is a good way to start*, Kate thought as she shivered slightly in the cold. It was almost as if the wind had run icy fingers down her back and whispered *I'm here* in her ear.

Then it was Annie's turn. As she invoked the south, standing with her hands over the flames, the firelight flickered over her face. "Creature of fire," she intoned. "Come join us in our circle, and bring with you the flame of passion."

Kate breathed in the smell of the smoke and let the fire warm her before she turned to face the sea. She held her hands out as if she were embracing the waves and the moon and the entire ocean.

"West!" she said. "Creature of water. Come join us in our circle tonight. Bring with you the depths of mystery."

Annie completed the circle by crying, "North!" in a strong voice. "Creature of earth. Come join us in our circle. Bring to us the strength of mountains." Kate felt the sand beneath her feet and looked at the rock walls of the cove, trying to feel the presence of the earth.

Facing each other again, they stood for a moment, listening to the sound of the waves and feeling the coldness of the night and the warmth of the fire. Then they sat on the sand around the fire. Kate opened her backpack, which she'd carried into the circle with her, and took out some things.

"I thought a lot about what kind of ritual we should do," she said. "This whole thing started because I asked for things I really shouldn't have asked for. So I thought that maybe I could stop what's been going on by giving some of those things back somehow. But I can't do it alone. That's why I asked you each to put something in the fire for me. We'll give them back by putting them into the fire and letting them burn."

Cooper went first. She held up a scrap of paper. "This is a piece of one of the Valentine's Day queen posters," she said. "You never should have tried to use magic to gain popularity." She threw the bit of poster onto the fire and they watched it burn up.

Annie went next. She also held up a piece of

paper. "This is your chemistry test," she said. "You should never have used magic to get this grade." She held the paper in the flames until it caught fire, then dropped the whole thing onto the burning driftwood.

Then it was Kate's turn. She held up the Ken doll, still wrapped in its red construction paper heart and tied with red ribbon. "This is the big one," she said, sighing. "I should have known better than to try to make someone fall in love with me." She took a pocketknife and cut the ribbon, unwinding it from around the doll. She took the ribbon and the paper heart with her name on it and held them in her hand over the flame. "So long," she said, dropping them into the fire.

They sat for a while watching the fire burn. Then Kate began to sing a chant she'd written for the ritual. She was nervous, and her voice faltered, but she got the words out.

"Fire crackling in the night, take what's wrong and make it right, burn away what we don't need, as is our will, so mote it be."

She sang the chant once more so that Annie and Cooper could learn the words, then their voices joined hers. They sang for quite some time. Kate shut her eyes and listened to the sound. It was soothing, almost hypnotic. Behind their words she heard the voice of the sea as the waves crashed on the beach, and she heard the wind as it sang in the rocks. All the sounds blended together perfectly, and she felt safe and happy.

One by one they stopped singing, until Kate was singing alone. She repeated the chant once more and let the last word hang in the air before dying away. She looked at her friends and smiled. "Now for the last part," she said.

She took the stick with the balloons tied to it and unwrapped the strings. She gave one to Annie and one to Cooper.

"I thought that since we were giving up things we . . . well, I . . . shouldn't have asked for, we should kind of start over by asking for more positive things," she explained. "Let's each think of something we would like to bring into our lives. Then we'll put those thoughts into the balloons and let them loose. You know, like sending out energy."

They took a few moments to think, holding the balloons in their hands. Then they stood up. Annie held out her balloon. "I wish I could worry less," she said. She let go of her balloon and it drifted up into the sky.

"I wish I could give people more of a chance," said Cooper, giving her balloon a little push and sending it off.

"And I wish I could be less afraid of changing," said Kate. She hesitated for a moment and then let go of her balloon quickly, before she could grab it back. As it sailed up toward the moon, she imagined her fears trailing behind it, leaving her forever.

"Do you think we'll get what we wished for?" Annie asked.

"We'll find out soon enough," Kate said. "But if there are any more mice in your kitchen when you get home, don't tell me about it."

CHAPTER 16

When Kate woke up the next morning something felt different. She couldn't tell exactly what it was, but she knew that there had been a change. As she got ready for school, she found herself humming a tune. After a while she realized that it was the chant she had written for the ceremony on the beach. She sang the words to herself as she dressed and thought about the ritual. The fire really had burned away a lot of the things that had been weighing her down. But what had it left behind? She definitely had a feeling of hope that she hadn't felt in a long time.

That hope faded a little as she walked to school. This was the big test. Had the ritual worked? She was about to find out. If it hadn't, she didn't know what she would do. She was out of ideas. Annie was still suspended, and if things kept going wrong, she was going to have a miserable time.

Some of the guys from the football team were hanging out on the steps when she arrived. She approached them nervously, waiting for their reaction to her. But when she walked by, they barely noticed. Only Evan Markson, Scott's best friend, waved at her, and even he went right back to talking to his buddies.

Maybe it's working, Kate thought as she entered the building. But she didn't dare hope for too much. She'd been fooled by the magic before, and there was a chance that it was just waiting to throw something even worse at her. As she walked to her locker she looked for any signs that the boys were still interested in her. She tensed up as each one walked by, waiting for one of them to ask her out or tell her how pretty she looked.

But none of them did, and by the time she reached her locker she was feeling a lot better. Still, she had the rest of the day to get through, so she wasn't going to consider the ritual a total success until she saw what happened. For the moment, it was time to face her next big challenge—the chemistry quiz.

Tara was sitting in her usual seat, going over her notes. "Hey," she said when Kate sat down. "Are you ready for this?"

"No," Kate admitted. "How about you?"

"I studied all last night," Tara said. "I have *got* to do well on this quiz. Coach Saliers says if I pass it she'll knock a couple of days off my suspension and let me play next week."

Kate pulled out her own notes and went over

them. Just to be fair, she had studied a little bit. If she did well on the quiz, she wanted it to be because she'd put in enough effort, and not because of magic.

She looked over her notes until Miss Blackwood came in and started handing out the quiz. When she got hers she turned it over and read through the questions. A few of them she knew, but many of them were totally unfamiliar to her. She remembered going over the material in her notes, but now it was all a blur.

Taking a deep breath, she tried to concentrate on the questions and see if the answers would come to her as they had on the midterm. But the more she looked at them, the more confused she got. The magic wasn't working.

She'd never been so happy to not know the answers to a quiz. She had to rely on her own knowledge, and she did the best she could. But when time ran out and Miss Blackwood asked for the papers back, she still had three blank places on her paper and was certain about only a few of the questions she had answered.

Miss Blackwood had them work on experiments for the remainder of class while she graded their tests. Kate paired up with Tara, and was relieved when the mixture they made fizzed up and poured over the sides of the beaker. It was the first time she'd been happy to have an experiment go wrong.

Miss Blackwood handed out the quizzes as the students left the room. Tara fidgeted nervously as she waited to get hers, and when the teacher gave it to her she let out a squeal of joy. "I passed!" she said. "That means I can play again."

Miss Blackwood handed Kate her test. "I'm afraid your news is not as good, Miss Morgan," she said. "I'm disappointed, especially after your midterm grade."

Kate looked at her paper. She'd gotten a 62. She tried to look upset, but inside she was celebrating. "I'll study harder for the next one," she told Miss Blackwood as she filed out into the hall. But what she really wanted to do was dance all the way to her next class.

At any other time, Kate would have called the day a total disaster. No one singled her out for attention. In addition to her failed chemistry quiz, she had trouble with a problem in math, couldn't get the colors to come out right on her art project, and in English class she picked the wrong Brontë sister when Mrs. Milder asked her to name the author of *Jane Eyre*. But instead of being depressed, Kate was elated. She felt normal again. Things weren't coming to her just because she'd done a spell. More and more, it seemed the ritual she had done with Cooper and Annie had worked.

Then it was time for lunch. As Kate entered the cafeteria, she realized that her biggest test was about to come. She hadn't seen Jessica or Sherrie all day, and she'd spent only one class period with Tara. She wondered how they would treat her. Walking toward their usual table, she forced herself to act casual.

"Hi, guys," she said, sitting down next to Sherrie.

"Hi," they said in unison.

"How's your costume coming for the dance?" Jess asked her.

"Fine," Kate said. "I just need to put the finishing touches on it. How about yours?"

"Almost done," Jessica said. "There's not a lot to do when you're wearing a nightgown and slippers."

"My Xena costume is great," said Tara. "I look like a real Amazon."

Kate waited for one of them to say something about her being queen, but none of them did. It was almost as if they'd forgotten she was even running.

"It's too bad *I'm* not running for queen," Sherrie said. "My Scarlett dress is to die for. I even have the accent down. I've seen *Gone with the Wind* so many times now I can practically recite it."

"Please don't," Tara said before Sherrie could begin.

"Oh, Kate," Jessica said. "We're all meeting at my house at six on Saturday for predance photos. You and Scott need to be there."

Scott. Kate had forgotten about Scott. More truthfully, she'd made herself not think about him. She hadn't seen him all day, and part of her hoped she wouldn't because she was so anxious about whether or not he'd still be into her. But no sooner had Jessica mentioned him than Kate looked up and saw him walking toward the table.

"Hi, Kate," he said.

"Hi, Scott," Sherrie said. "We were just talking about you. Are you all set to escort our little Kate to the big dance?"

"Well, I sort of need to talk to you about that," Scott said, looking at Kate. "I don't think I'm going to be able to go."

Kate felt her stomach clench. She had been afraid that something like this would happen. She knew she had asked for too much when she did the spell to get Scott's attention. Now that the power of the magic was gone, she knew she would lose him.

"Not go?" said Tara, sounding mad. "Don't tell me you're dumping our best friend?"

"That's right," added Jessica. "If you hurt her feelings, you'll have us to answer to."

Kate was surprised to hear her friends standing up for her like this. She was even more surprised when Scott said, "No, of course not. It's just that this football scout called me and wants me to come talk to the coach at his university about a scholarship there next year. It's the only weekend they can do it, so I can't say no. It's a really big deal. But I promise I'll make it up to her. We'll have our own Valentine's Day next weekend— something romantic. Really, Kate, I want to go to the dance with you more than anything. But this is a big chance for me."

"I say kick him to the curb," said Sherrie to Kate. "If football is more important than Valentine's Day, then I think someone's priorities are a little screwed up."

Kate looked at Scott. He was giving her a sad puppy dog look that she couldn't resist. "It's okay," she said, weak-kneed with relief. "A scholarship is more important than a dance. And we can do something next week."

Scott beamed. "I knew you'd understand," he said. "I told the guys I had the best girlfriend around." Before Kate knew what was happening, he leaned over and kissed her for a long moment, then pulled away. "I've got to go talk to Coach about getting my stats for the university, but I'll call you tonight, okay?"

Kate nodded, speechless. She was still remembering how his lips had felt on hers and how he had called her his girlfriend. *And me with peanut butter breath*, she thought. It wasn't exactly how she'd imagined their first kiss would be, but it was one she would never forget. And given that she'd expected Scott to break up with her once the spell was over, it was the best first kiss she could've dreamed of.

"That was so sweet," Jessica said, sighing.

"But now who are you going to go to the dance with?" Sherrie asked, as usual turning a good moment into a downer.

But Kate wasn't about to let Sherrie get to her.

She put her arm around her and hugged her. "Who needs a date when they've got Scarlett, Xena, and Wendy for best friends?" she said.

Kate couldn't wait to talk to Annie and Cooper and tell them what had happened. Then she remembered that Annie was still stuck at home. But there was still Cooper, and Kate got her chance before her history class, when they all ran into each other in the second-floor hallway.

"What do you think the thing with Scott means?" she asked.

"That you have really bad taste in men?" Cooper suggested.

"I mean about the magic," Kate said, making a face. "Shouldn't he be ignoring me again like all the other guys?"

Cooper looked thoughtful. "Maybe it wasn't just the magic," she said. "That's what got his attention, but maybe once he got to know you better he saw something he liked. That part might have stayed behind even when the spell was broken." She paused before adding, "Or maybe he's just a stupid football player."

"Do I make fun of your boyfriend?" Kate said. "Oh, wait, you don't have one."

"But you would if I did," Cooper said, and they both laughed.

"I just can't believe he's still around," Kate said. "I thought for sure everything would go back to the way it was before I opened that book."

"Including not being friends with me and Annie?" Cooper asked.

"Not that part," Kate said. "That's the other good thing that came from this whole mess." She corrected herself, "The best thing. Now if we can just get Annie back here, we'll be all set."

"I'm glad you feel that way," said Cooper. "Annie and I were talking, and we want to make this a regular thing."

"Make what a regular thing?" Kate asked.

"The circles," said Cooper. "We think it would be fun to learn more about all of this. We should probably stay away from spells for a while, but there's a lot of other stuff we can do."

The excitement Kate had been feeling ever since Scott's kiss melted away a little. "I don't know," she said. "I don't know if I can."

"Come on," said Cooper. "Didn't last night mean anything to you?"

"Sure it did," Kate said. "It was great. But I just assumed it would be the last time. You know, tying up loose ends and all of that."

"So now that no one is mad at you anymore and you still have your boyfriend, you don't want to upset the balance, is that it?" Cooper said.

Kate didn't say anything. Cooper was exactly right. Yes, she had enjoyed the ritual. Yes, she found Wicca interesting. But could she risk getting too involved again? She didn't know.

"I have to think about it," she said.

"Well, we're getting together tomorrow night at Annie's house," Cooper said. "I hope you'll come."

The first bell rang for the next class, and they left the room. As they stepped into the hall, they found themselves almost bumping into Terri Fletcher, who was hobbling along on crutches accompanied by two of her friends carrying her books. When Cooper and Kate saw her, they froze.

Terri looked at them. "I was hoping I'd run into you guys," she said.

Cooper glanced at Kate nervously. Neither of them said anything.

"I want to apologize," Terri said.

"Apologize?" Kate said. "For what?"

"When I fell, I was in a lot of pain and I was really embarrassed," Terri said. "I wanted to blame someone for my accident, and Annie was the person I took it out on. I really did convince myself that she must have pushed me because she was near me. But the janitor told Mrs. Browning that he had just waxed those steps, and the more I thought about it the more I realized that I only slipped."

"So Annie isn't suspended anymore?" Cooper asked doubtfully.

"My parents withdrew their complaint," Terri said. "She should be here tomorrow."

Kate couldn't believe what was happening. It was like some weird Disney movie where everyone lived happily ever after. All they needed were some singing birds and mice wearing hats. As Terri lurched off to her class, Kate turned to Cooper. "Did we do all this?" she asked.

"It looks that way," Cooper said. "I guess when we cleaned house last night we really cleaned house. Maybe you've got more witchiness in you than you think you do."

"Don't start," said Kate. "I already told you, I think my witching days are behind me."

They went to their separate classes, and Kate didn't see Cooper for the rest of the day. After basketball practice, Kate went out with Sherrie, Tara, and Jessica for hamburgers. It felt strange to not be talking about magic or witchcraft or anything except clothes, boys, and the usual teenage things. A couple of times Kate wanted to ask her friends what they thought about Wicca, but every time she started to say something she ended up talking about Britney Spears or the new Jennifer Love Hewitt movie or something else unimportant.

When she got home that night, Scott called and they talked for a long time. He was very excited about his upcoming trip and spent a lot of time describing the university's football program to Kate. Then they talked about their plans for when he got back, plans Kate hoped would include a peanut-butter-free kiss.

After Kate hung up she sat on her bed and thought. She should have been totally happy. Everything was working out. No one was mad at her. She had a great boyfriend. She'd successfully put an end to the chaos caused by her spells.

But something was missing. Some part of her still wasn't satisfied, and she couldn't quite figure out what it was. She picked up the Tarot card that Archer had given her and looked at the three women holding up their cups. Then it came to her. *She* hadn't put an end to the problems her spells had caused. She'd needed Annie's and Cooper's help. They'd done it together, as a group.

She thought back to the day when she'd first approached Annie. She'd been so nervous. She hadn't had any idea how Annie would react. And talking to Cooper had been even harder. But she'd done it. They'd all done it.

She realized that *that* was what was missing. She needed Cooper and Annie. And not just as friends she said hello to in the halls or did things with sometimes. She needed to be with them in a magic circle, feeling the energy the way she'd felt it in Annie's room and on the beach.

She was still afraid. She didn't know what continuing to explore Wicca would mean. And, she told herself, she still might decide it wasn't for her. But she knew she had to give it a try. She picked up the phone and dialed. When Cooper answered Kate said, "I'll be there tomorrow night," then hung up before she could change her mind.

CHAPTER 17

Friday was so busy that Kate barely had time to think. Because she was on the dance planning committee, she was excused from all of her classes so that she could help get things ready. Sherrie was, as always, in charge, and she had everyone running around in a frenzy of putting up decorations, making banners, and doing a hundred other things all at once.

Kate was assigned to decoration duty. She and Tara had the job of putting white, blue, and pink paper on every visible surface in the gym and then hanging streamers from anything they could reach.

"This is supposed to be a fairy tale castle, people!" Sherrie kept shouting. "I want to see magic!"

"Yeah, it's a fairy tale castle all right," Tara said as she and Kate taped what seemed to be the four thousandth streamer to the basketball backdrop. "And I know who the wicked witch is."

Kate laughed, but she wondered what Tara would say if she knew what she'd been up to. Would

Tara think *Kate* was a wicked witch? Kate cut another streamer and pushed the thought to the back of her mind.

Sherrie had gotten some of the kids from the drama club to paint backdrops for the dance, and they were busily constructing a castle entrance around the gym door. The school handyman and his helpers were stringing white lights from the ceiling, and other volunteers were setting up small circular tables all around the gym floor.

All day Kate worked on the dance preparations. They even worked after hours, taking a quick break to eat pizza that was delivered. When it was time to go home the gym had been transformed, and Kate felt like Cinderella after a long day of doing the chores her stepmother set out for her. But she had one more thing to do before she was done for the day.

When she arrived at the Crandall house, her two friends were up in Annie's room. Kate walked in and threw herself down on Annie's bed.

"I don't ever want to see another piece of crepe paper again," she said.

"You're the one who wants to be a normal high school girl," Cooper said. "If you want to be normal, you have to take the crepe paper."

"You know," said Kate, sitting up, "you could use a little dose of normal yourself. It wouldn't hurt you to expand your horizons an inch or two, either."

"Please," Cooper said. "I do *not* need to experience the thrill of five hundred people in silly outfits crammed into a room that smells like sweaty feet while some cover band plays 'My Heart Will Go On' and everyone gets all weepy."

Annie giggled. "You make it sound so appealing," she said.

"Have either of you ever been to a dance?" Kate asked.

Annie shook her head. Cooper snorted derisively. "Not on your life," she said.

Kate smiled. "Then I'll make you a deal."

"A deal?" Cooper said. "What are you talking about?"

"You two want me to be part of this . . . whatever we're calling it, right? Our little Wiccan study group."

"Yeah," Cooper said suspiciously.

"What are you thinking?" Annie asked, looking nervous.

"I'll do it," Kate said. "On one condition. You two have to come to the dance with me tomorrow."

"No way!" Cooper shrieked. "I wouldn't be caught dead at that thing."

"I couldn't," said Annie, looking horrified.

"That's the deal," Kate said. "Take it or leave it. If you want me to be part of this group, you have to be part of mine for one night. Besides, I don't have a date."

Cooper was fuming. "I can't believe you would

do something so horrible," she said. "This is just wrong."

"Then you'll do it?" Kate asked sweetly.

Cooper looked at Annie. "What do you say?" she asked.

Annie sighed. "We could just try to turn her into a toad," she said.

"I'll take that as a yes," said Kate. "Now, let's talk about costumes."

"Costumes later," said Cooper. "Business first. We haven't really discussed what we want to do. Does anyone have any ideas?"

"I've been thinking about it a lot," Annie said. "I've also been reading up on some things in the books I got at the bookstore, and I have a proposal."

"Propose away," said Kate.

"I think we need to start small," Annie said. "Trying to do too much at once is what got us into trouble in the first place."

"So where do we begin?" asked Cooper. "What is there besides spells and moons and candles and all of that?"

"A lot," said Annie. "There's the Goddess, for one thing. And the God, too. And the esbats."

"The whats?" Kate said.

"Esbats," Annie repeated. "The full moons. Witches celebrate the full moons. Like we did last night. Only there's a lot about the moon's cycles we haven't even started to explore. And then there are the sabbats."

"More moons?" Cooper said.

Annie shook her head. "They're kind of like Wiccan holidays. They're special days that celebrate different times of the year. Like Samhain and Yule."

"Enough with the foreign language already," Cooper said. "Speak English."

"I thought you knew all about this stuff," Kate said to Cooper. "Didn't your grandmother tell you any of this?"

"No way," Cooper said. "She was just into protection spells and folk magic. This is all new to me."

"It's all part of Wicca," Annie said. "Like Sophia said, this is a religion, not a hobby. It's a lot more complicated than just doing some rituals. I think we really need to study this stuff and find out what it's all about."

"But our ritual last night worked," Kate said. "Why do more than we have to?"

"Because just being able to do spells isn't all there is," Annie said. "I think there are some really interesting things we're missing. If we start at the beginning, we can do it right. And then who knows what kind of spells we'll be able to do."

"Okay," said Cooper. "Let's give it a shot. Witch school is officially open."

"Kate?" Annie said.

Kate looked from Cooper to Annie. "You'll really go to the dance tomorrow?" she asked.

"Promise," said Cooper.

"Promise," echoed Annie.

"All right then," Kate said. "It's a deal. Now, let's talk about outfits. I have a great idea."

On Saturday, Kate put the finishing touches on her costume. She'd had to make a few adjustments to it since Annie and Cooper had agreed to go with her, but when she was done she was pleased with the results. At a little before six she went over to Jessica's house for the photo session. Her friends and their dates were all there, looking great in their costumes and showing off for one another.

"Nice tights," Kate said to Blair Peterson, who was dressed as Peter Pan. Jessica, in her Wendy outfit, was running around with the camera snapping pictures.

"It's one of the advantages of taking ballet class," Blair said.

"Doesn't Al make a great Ares?" Tara said, marching up in her Xena garb. "We even painted a beard on with mascara. Just don't tell Sherrie. It was hers and we used it up."

"Very Greek god," Kate commented. "And I love your armor."

Sherrie and Sean were parading around as Rhett and Scarlett. Sherrie even had a big frilly parasol that she carried over her shoulder. "Ah do declah," she said in a terrible imitation of a Southern accent. "Wherever is your costume, Kate?"

Kate had come dressed in jeans and a sweater. She held up the bag she was carrying. "It's in here," she said. "I want it to be a surprise."

"You have to stand in the middle then," Jessica said as she arranged the group for their photos. "That way no one will notice that you're not dressed up."

Kate took her place, standing in between Sherrie and Jessica. Jessica gave the camera to her father, and he snapped a series of pictures while they all tried to hold their smiles.

"I can't wait to see what this costume of yours is," Tara said as they all climbed into Jessica's father's minivan for the ride to school.

Kate hugged the bag to her chest and didn't say anything. Although she was excited about what she was about to do, she was also really nervous. But she was determined to go through with it. When they arrived at school she excused herself and went to the girl's bathroom. Annie and Cooper were already there.

"You guys look great!" Kate said, making them turn around to show her their costumes.

"I can't believe you're making us do this," Cooper said. "I feel like an idiot."

"You look fabulous," Kate said. "Now, wait for me while I get changed."

When Kate was ready the three girls walked to the gym entrance, where couples were lined up to go inside. A boy at the door was taking names, and when the couples walked in the names of their characters were announced. Kate hung back so her other friends wouldn't see her standing there with Annie and Cooper. Luckily, they were too busy talking and worrying about their own costumes to notice anything else.

"Miss Scarlett O'Hara and Mr. Rhett Butler," the boy said, and Sherrie and Sean walked into the dance to the sound of applause.

One by one the couples entered. As it came time for Kate, Annie, and Cooper to enter, the boy with the list approached them. "And you are?" he asked.

Kate told him and he wrote down their names. Then it was their turn to go in. "Ready?" Kate asked Cooper and Annie.

"As I'll ever be," Cooper said as they all took deep breaths.

"Presenting the good fairies Flora, Fauna, and Merryweather," the announcer said, and the girls walked into the dance.

As they entered, people turned to look. Then they began to clap.

"Great costumes!" someone yelled.

Kate looked at Annie and Cooper. They were dressed as Sleeping Beauty's three fairy godmothers. Kate wore a blue dress, Annie's was green, and Cooper's was bright pink. They also wore tall, pointed hats and carried magic wands that Kate had made that morning.

"I feel like a birthday cake," Cooper said as the girls moved into the room to make way for the next group of people. "Which one am I supposed to be again?"

"Flora," Kate said. "Annie is Fauna. And I'm Merryweather."

Kate scanned the room for Sherrie, Jessica, and Tara. She knew she couldn't hide from them forever. Eventually they would see her, and unless they were totally blind they would probably notice that she, Annie, and Cooper were wearing similar costumes. She hadn't decided yet what she would do if they asked her why they were dressed similarly. She knew that her two groups of friends would probably never mix, and she knew that she was going to have a difficult time explaining to Sherrie, Jessica, and Tara why she wanted to spend time with Cooper and Annie. But that could wait. She was going to enjoy herself for as long as she could.

She looked around. With the white lights twinkling, the tables set with flowers, and the band playing, it really did feel like they were in an enchanted ballroom. All around them were couples dressed in different outfits, as though they had been transformed right along with the gym into something magical, at least for one night.

"I'm sorry Scott couldn't come with you," Annie said as they went to the refreshments table and got something to drink.

"Not half as sorry as I am," said Cooper. "If any of my other friends see me in this getup my reputation will be shot."

"Get over it," said Kate. "If anyone gives you any trouble, just smack them with your wand."

She took a bite of a cookie and chewed on it. "I'm glad Scott couldn't come," she said. "I can see him any time. But how often do I get to go out dancing with my fairy godsisters?"

As they were standing around talking a trumpet sounded, startling them. On the stage stood a boy dressed as a royal page. When he had everyone's attention he held up an envelope.

"As you all know," he said. "We've been taking votes for Valentine's Day queen this week. We had a record turnout this year, and the race was close. But we have a winner, and it's time to announce her name."

"I forgot all about the queen thing," Kate said, starting to feel slightly sick. "I wonder if we turned the spell back in time to stop something awful from happening."

The boy opened the envelope and pulled out a piece of paper. The crowd was silent as they waited for him to read the name of the winner.

"This year's Valentine's Day queen is," he began. Kate held her breath. It seemed to take forever for the boy to finish his announcement. "Terri Fletcher," he said.

A spotlight searched the crowd, landing on the table where Terri sat with her friends. Her hand was over her mouth, and her friends were hugging her. Finally she stood and limped to the stage.

"I don't know what to say," she said as someone handed her a microphone.

"Who's your king?" someone called out.

Kate held her breath, wondering what Terri would say. After all, if it hadn't been for her, Terri would be at the dance with Scott. Did Terri still hold a grudge about how things had turned out, or had the magic taken care of that, too?

But Terri just laughed. "I guess I don't have one," she said. "Are there any volunteers?"

Several guys rushed forward toward the stage, with Jeff Higdon reaching it first. Taking Terri's hand, he led her down the steps and onto the dance floor.

The band started to play, and as Terri and Jeff danced together a group of guys from the football team, all dressed as cupids, ran out and showered them with little red paper hearts.

"I think I'm going to be sick," Cooper said.

"I think it's sweet," said Annie, and Kate and Cooper looked at her in surprise.

"Well, that's the last of the magic," Kate said. "Everything is wrapped up and out of the way. Now it's on to bigger and better things."

She held up her glass. "I'd like to make a toast," she said. "To magic."

Annie lifted her glass beside Kate's. "To magic," she said.

Cooper added her cup to the other two. "To magic," she said.

They stood there for a moment under the twinkling lights, the sound of the band and the noise of the crowd surrounding them. Kate looked up at their three hands holding the cups and thought once more of the final card in her Tarot reading. Archer had said that the Three of Cups represented the perfection of friendship and the beginning of something special. She knew that Annie and Cooper had come into her life for an important reason, and in a short time they had become good friends she felt she could trust. She had thought of their ritual as being the end of something, but maybe she'd been wrong.

"Well, it's not Princess Aurora or Maleficent," a strident voice broke in. "But it's the next best thing."

Kate looked over and saw Sherrie staring at her. Sherrie took in the three of them holding up their cups, and a cold smile spread across her face.

"My, my, my," she said as she picked up the edge of her skirt and turned to go. "Just wait until the girls hear about this."

follow the

circle of three

with book 2: merry meet

"You're fifteen minutes late, young lady," added Cooper, her arms across her chest in mock annoyance.

"Sorry, moms," Kate said, pushing past her two friends and walking straight into the kitchen, where she knew there would be some hot chocolate waiting for her. Annie's rambling old house had become her second home, and Kate even had her own mug that she used whenever she came over.

"I can't believe you're not giving us the deets," Annie said plaintively, coming in right behind her.

"Deets?" said Kate, putting her backpack down and taking off her coat.

"You know, details," Annie explained.

"Since when did you get all streetwise?" Kate asked, pulling out a chair and sitting down at the kitchen table.

First things first," said Cooper. "We have something to show you."

Kate looked from Cooper to Annie. Sometimes she couldn't believe that the three of them were really friends. Kate was as outgoing as Annie was shy. And Cooper, with her ever-changing hair color (it had recently gone from bright pink to bright blue) and loner attitude, was the last person Kate would have ever thought she'd be spending a Friday night with. But that, too, was before the whole spell thing. Now here she was, waiting for Cooper and Annie to spill the beans.

"While you were out with lover boy, Annie and I made a trip down to Crones' Circle," Cooper said, referring to the funky bookstore where the three of them had been spending a lot of time since their experience with the spell book the month before. The store specialized in books about Wicca and other esoteric topics, and they had learned a lot since first walking through the door in search of some much-needed help.

"And?" Kate said with exaggerated effect.

"And we found this," Cooper said, handing Kate a flyer printed on grass-green paper.

Kate took the flyer and looked at it, reading it out loud as she munched on a cookie. "'The Coven of the Green Wood invites you to a celebration of the Spring Equinox. Saturday, March 19. Ritual begins at five, with potluck after. Bring food to share.'"

"Doesn't it sound great?" Annie asked excitedly. "It's an open ritual. Anyone can go."

"Sophia said it would be okay if we came," Cooper added. Sophia was one of the women who owned Crones' Circle, and she had answered many of their questions about Wicca.

"I don't know," said Kate, staring at the flyer.

"What do you mean you don't know?" Cooper said irritably. "It's our first ritual."

"First one with real witches," Annie corrected.

Kate looked from one to the other. They both seemed so excited. She wished she was as sure as they seemed to be. Getting together with real witches made everything feel a lot more serious, at least to Kate, who still wasn't entirely sure what she thought about the whole subject of Wicca. She didn't know if she was ready for it.

"I'll think about it," she said, and her friends groaned. They knew that whenever Kate said she'd think about something it really meant she didn't want to do it but was afraid to hurt their feelings.

"Think fast," Cooper said. "It's tomorrow night."

"Tomorrow is tomorrow," Kate said, thinking about what Scott had said earlier in the evening. "We have lots of time. Now, don't you want to hear about this ring?"

circle of three

isobel bird

join the circle...

book 2: merry meet

Joined by an uneasy bond, Kate, Cooper, and Annie
are resolved to explore their newfound fascination
with witchcraft. The three very different girls
attend an open pagan ritual, and while each is
drawn to the power of witches, it becomes appar-
ent that they must come together as three before
they might begin to learn the ways of Wicca.

0-06-447292-2

book 3: second sight

As Annie, Cooper, and Kate begin to learn the
Craft, a girl in their town goes missing. Cooper has
what she thinks are nightmares about it—until it
becomes clear that she is having visions about what
really happened to the girl. Cooper knows what
she must do, but is terrified that it will mean
revealing the secret she and her friends have kept
until now.

0-06-447293-0